IN THE WILDS OF TEXAS,
EVIL RIDES THE RAILS . . .

Longarm was halfway down the steps, looking left and right and straight ahead for Meadows, when a bullet suddenly zinged by his ear and buried itself in the ground at the bottom of the steps. He instantly jumped back, realizing it was the sentry on the roof. He transferred his revolver to his right hand and fired into the ceiling, not knowing if a bullet would penetrate or not.

Almost instantly he heard a bang from above him and a bullet came tearing through the ceiling, struck the metal floor, and ricocheted off into the other door. Without pause Longarm pointed Meadows's .45-caliber revolver at the hole the rifle bullet had made and fired three quick shots. For a second he thought nothing had happened, but then he heard a strangled cry, and turned just in time to see the trooper come falling by the open door and hit the ground with a thump. He lay still, and Longarm could see blood staining the blue of his uniform pants at the crotch.

"Damn!" he said. *Hell of a place to get hit . . .*

TABOR EVANS

LONGARM

AND THE TEXAS HIJACKERS

JOVE BOOKS, NEW YORK

LONGARM AND THE TEXAS HIJACKERS

A Jove Book / published by arrangement with
the author

PRINTING HISTORY
Jove edition / November 1994

ISBN: 0-515-11493-6

A JOVE BOOK®
Jove Books are published by The Berkley Publishing Group,
200 Madison Avenue, New York, New York 10016.
JOVE and the "J" design are trademarks
belonging to Jove Publications, Inc.

PRINTED IN THE UNITED STATES OF AMERICA

10 9 8 7 6 5 4 3 2 1

9/30/04

Chapter 1

Deputy U.S. Marshal Custis Long lay in the middle of Molly
Coy's bed in her back bedroom in Broken Bow, Oklahoma
Territory. He was on his back and Molly was lying beside
him on her side, running the tips of her fingers slowly up and
down his body from his neck to his ears. Both were naked. It
was ten in the morning and, except when Molly had gotten
up about eight to make coffee and scramble them some eggs,
they'd been in bed since nine the previous night.

Molly Coy was a striking-looking woman on the young
side of thirty who had flaming red hair and soft creamy
skin that made the rosettes of her nipples seem all the more
scarlet—like wild strawberries, Longarm thought, admiring
them. Molly was the widow of one of his best friends, Mack
Coy. Mack had also been a deputy U.S. marshal, and had
been killed by bandits some four years past in that same
Oklahoma Territory where he'd been headquartered. Even
though Longarm was headquartered out of Denver, they had
worked on many a job together. He'd known Molly ever
since Mack had married her as a young girl of nineteen, and
had kept on knowing her through their marriage and after
Mack's death. Molly had turned to him in her grief because

1

he'd been Mack's friend, and because he understood what being the wife of a deputy marshal meant. One day she had just come into his arms, in a natural way, out of a need for the kind of comfort that words and gentle hugs couldn't give. From then on it had been an easy step to intimate lovemaking whenever the chance came along.

Molly had never remarried, even though half the men in the Territory would have given her their cattle for the chance to court her. But as she'd told Longarm one time, "After Mack they wouldn't seem like much. No, I'd rather just go along like I am." She'd been curled up in his arms at the time and she'd reached up to caress his cheek with her soft fingers. "Besides, I've got you for this. And you come around enough to keep me satisfied." She'd smiled. "Almost. You just got to be sure you get my jug filled to the brim every time."

So, since the previous night, they'd been trying to make sure Longarm didn't go off leaving her half full. He had a train leaving in four hours, and he wasn't sure he was going to have strength to make it.

Broken Bow was a rail town on the route from Fort Smith, Arkansas, to Tulsa. Longarm was on his way to Texas, but he'd swung out of his way to spend time with Molly, a thing he often did when circumstances allowed. She ran a boardinghouse, more for the comfort of the constant company, Longarm suspected, than out of need for the money. The wife of a deputy marshal had a lonely life, and she sometimes joked that she saw as much of Longarm as she had of Mack when he'd been alive. But Molly wasn't a woman to complain about a bargain after she'd made it, and she hadn't complained about her life as a marshal's wife anymore than she'd complained when Longarm had told her, when he'd come in the night before, that he couldn't stay but that one night. He'd said, "And truth be told, I'm stretching it stopping off like this. Billy Vail would have a hissy fit if he knew what I was doing."

She'd said, "The hell with Billy Vail," and had kissed him and taken him by the hand and led him back to the softness of her and her bed.

Now she leaned over and began kissing him lightly in the places her fingers had stimulated. Without warning she suddenly took him in her mouth. He let out a little moan, and then a sigh as she used her tongue to coax him into full erectness. He was already beginning to tremble as she got up on her knees and swung one leg over and straddled him. She took him with her hand and guided him inside herself. She was slick and warm, and he involuntarily arched his back as she began rocking back and forth, pumping him up and down, making him feel as if she was swallowing him whole. She leaned forward, putting her mouth on his, her tongue questing and searching. He took her buttocks in both of his big hands and rocked her back and forth, up and down, the tempo slowly increasing. Their breaths were coming faster and faster, their bodies joined in such a fierce embrace that it seemed they must fuse together. He felt the heat rising in him, felt that surge, like a giant wave, dimly heard her gasping, felt her fingers digging into his shoulders and back.

And then there was an explosion and it seemed as if they both rose up in the air over the bed. Longarm could feel his strength pumping out of him, feel himself going downward, feel the last of his energy being spent in faint gasps.

For a little while she lay on top of him, her breath soft and warm in his ear. Then, inch by inch, she slowly slid off to the side of him and lay on the bed, one of her breasts just resting on his chest.

When he could, Longarm said, "Molly, honey, I hope your jug is full because this old man is out of milk. You have drained me dry."

3

She got up on one elbow and kissed him on the cheek. "You're a sweet man, Custis Long. I hate that nickname of yours. Longarm. The long arm of the law. Whose bright idea was that?"

"I forgot," Longarm said. He turned his head to the right so he could see down the length of her body. Even with his passion spent, Molly's body was still a treat to look at with her soft, rounded curves, her creamy skin, and her beautifully shaped, slightly drooping breasts that were such a pleasure to fondle with their large ruby nipples and big rosettes. She had a soft, rounded belly that tapered down into a mound covered with a silky flaming bush that disappeared between her velvet-skinned thighs. He had told her once that her bush looked like a small hill suffering from a prairie fire.

She said, "I best get up. I've got to fry up some chicken for my boarders. I'll make plenty so you can take some with you on the train. What time do you have to leave?"

He yawned. "Sooner than I want to. Train gets in here at two. I got to be on it."

Still on her left elbow, she ran her hands over his hard, lean body, stopping to feel the white scars on his chest and his side and a big one on his right thigh. She said, "Custis, for God's sake, there seems to be more of them every time I see you. How many times have you been shot and stabbed?"

He sighed. "More than I needed to be."

She touched an ugly scar on his left breast. "This one should have killed you."

"That's what the doc said." He paused, thinking about the time he'd either been too trusting or too careless and let an outlaw press a hideout gun into him. He'd never let that happen again. He said, "If there was any justice or penalty for stupidity, it would have. Or should have."

4

He was somewhere around six feet tall. He didn't know exactly because there had never been any occasion to measure himself. All he knew was that he seldom had to look up to meet someone's eyes. He was heavy in the shoulders and arms, with big hands and slim, hard legs. His face, sometimes, said he was in his thirties, but there were other times when it was weighed down with fatigue and worry and could have passed for forty. He didn't pay much attention to such matters as age or other measurements. His only measure was did he get the job done and did he get it done like it ought to get done. He was not a man for small matters or trivialities. When someone would ask how long he'd been a deputy U.S., marshal, he'd simply answer by saying he didn't know and didn't much care. "Somebody is keeping count and they'll let me know when it's time to go to pasture. Till then I'll just keep following orders."

Which was a statement that always made Billy Vail, his boss and the chief marshal for the Colorado district, laugh. Billy said that the only time Longarm followed orders was whenever Longarm's notions and the orders just happened to coincide.

Molly got out of bed, went to a bureau in the corner, and took down a loose-fitting robe that she tied with a sash. Then she stood in front of a mirror for a moment brushing her hair. Longarm swung around, put his feet on the floor, and sat on the side of the bed watching her. He said, "Molly, wasn't nobody asked me, but I see something mighty fine going to waste. Was ever a woman made to be a wife and please a man, it was you, and I don't care what room of the house we are talking about—kitchen, living room, bedroom."

She put the brush away and turned for the door. "We've talked about that. You know how I feel."

He caught her by the robe as she passed by and pulled her to him. The sash fell off and the robe opened. He kissed

5

her on her small navel and then leaned his head against her soft belly. He said, "Why haven't I asked you to marry me, Molly? I ain't afraid of being told no. I've heard that before, though never to that particular question. But I can't go on with this life forever, and I shore couldn't do no better than you."

She laughed and put her arms around his head and hugged her to him. She said, "My God, Custis, you have such style. You don't want to get married because you'd have to give up all your girlfriends."

He protested, "I ain't got no girlfriends."

"Don't tell me, Custis Long. Why, if we was married I wouldn't let you out of the house without sewing the fly of your jeans shut."

He smiled into the softness of her belly. "That might get inconvenient at times."

She hugged his head again. "Thank you for the thought, Custis. You're a dear, sweet man. I don't know how you can be so hard and tough and still be gentle. Maybe you could replace Mack. You're the only one I think that could. But . . ." She pulled back and looked down until he raised his face to her. "But you're still a deputy federal marshal. You may be better than Mack was. Probably you are because you've lasted longer. But even you could get bushwhacked or shot in the back. It's too dangerous. Too dangerous for me. I couldn't go through that pain again." She leaned down and kissed him lightly. "When you put that badge down and choose where you go and why, then come and let's talk about it. Meanwhile, I'll fix you an early lunch. I've got a side of beef in the icehouse. I'll cut you off a steak."

When she was gone he slowly got dressed. He was wearing jeans and a cotton shirt. He had two more shirts and an extra pair of jeans in his saddlebags, which lay in the corner. It was mid-July and hot and he was traveling without

6

a jacket or even underwear, which he'd come to wear only in the winter or when he had to go into the mountains. The only other articles in his saddlebags were two bottles of good whiskey, an extra three pairs of socks, and two boxes of .44-caliber ammunition, along with his spare revolver, a Colt .44 with a nine-inch barrel. In the holster hanging from the bedpost was the Colt .44 he carried for general use. It had a six-inch barrel and was more suited to everyday work. He only carried the Colt with the nine-inch barrel for the few occasions that came along where he needed greater accuracy in a handgun at longer range.

In his left boot, in a secure little pocket he'd had sewn in there, he carried a slim little dagger that he could throw with fair accuracy. He'd only had to use it once, but it had come in mighty handy on that occasion. Billy Vail had once asked him why he carried so many "doodads," and he'd said, "Well, Billy, I might not ever need them. But when I do I'm gonna need them mighty bad."

Custis Long was not a man who liked to leave much to chance. He believed in doing his gambling at the poker table. His work was too serious to trust to luck.

When he was dressed he stamped his boots on the hardwood floor of the bedroom to get his feet settled in, and then headed for the kitchen to find Molly.

Molly sat with him and watched while he ate, contenting herself with a cup of coffee and a glass of well-watered whiskey. She'd eat later, if she ate at all, when her boarders came in. Broken Bow was a railroad division point, so all her roomers and boarders were train crewmen. It was the end of their run. They'd get in, stay the night at Molly's, and then head back the way they'd come on the return train. The arriving crew would take their place. Since the railroad contracted with Molly for food and beds, she never had any trouble collecting her bills. "Ain't nobody pays like the railroads," she now said.

Longarm said, "They ought to. God knows they got the money."

"Tell me about this job Billy Vail has sent you on. You're going after cavalry deserters? Isn't that the army's business?"

"At first glance you'd think so, but this one is a little different. Was eight of them deserted, and one of them was an officer, a second lieutenant."

Molly looked surprised. "An officer? I've never heard of an officer deserting. I thought they could resign their commission or something."

Longarm shrugged. "They can, after their first parcel of duty, which I believe to be four years. And this one, this lieutenant, had in six or seven years. Nobody can make heads or tails of it, but it appears to be so. At first it was thought that the other seven, the enlisted men, had taken him along as a hostage, but then the bunch held up a bank in San Angelo, Texas, still wearing their uniforms, and it was clear that this here lieutenant was running the show."

She shook her head. "That's strange."

"Yep." Longarm got out a little cigar, dug out a match, and lit it. "They deserted from Fort Davis, which is clean on out in west Texas. I've seen that country, and I've had a hangover so bad I'd have paid a man to shoot me. On the whole I'd rather live with the hangover than that country around Fort Davis."

"Think that was why the officer deserted? Or all of them?"

"Naw." Longarm took a moment to relight his cigar. "All that bunch had been serving out there long enough they could have gotten transfers. There's still Apache trouble out there, and these were some of the best Indian fighters

8

that cavalry detachment had. It figures they've taken to a life of crime on purpose. I reckon they figure it pays better than the army. But God knows, they are going to be hell to run down and hem up. Every one of them is a well-trained and disciplined soldier, and their leader is experienced. It's not going to be like trying to take some gang of ragamuffins into custody. These boys are going to be organized and smart. Makes them that much more dangerous."

She looked at him a long moment as if thinking about his semi-proposal of marriage. "And so you're going after them. That makes a lot of sense. Eight-to-one odds."

He smiled. "It ain't like you think, Molly. It seems that the army has got to do things in bunches of men and ain't no bunch of men going to slip up on these boys. So my job is just to locate them and then send for the cavalry. I know you were thinking I'd turned foolhardy in my old age, but I ain't that crazy. These boys are armed with that brand-new Springfield rifle that fires five bullets in a clip bolt-action. They say it is accurate up to a thousand yards. I reckon that is an exaggeration by the Springfield company, but even half that distance makes it dangerous. No, I'm just on a tracking job. I'll go to Fort Davis and get a line on the men from their friends and commanders, and then go to San Angelo and talk to the people at the bank. The bank holdup alone kind of draws me into it. But the real reason I got sent is that I'm supposed to be able to move around and gather information without being noticed. At least that's what Billy Vail said. Maybe he just thought I'd had it easy for too long. I been beating him at poker a little too regular."

"What was the officer's name? Do you have any particulars about him?"

"Not a whole lot. His name is James Meadows. Nobody was ever heard to call him Jim. He's described as a pretty sober kind of fellow, and I'm not talking about whiskey, though it's known he never takes a drink. That right there worries me. He is twenty-eight years of age, and has been in the cavalry some six or seven years. He wasn't raised and educated to be an officer and a gentleman. For the first four years of his military life he was an enlisted man. But then, a couple of years ago, he pulled some sort of heroic deed— rescued his commander through a hail of bullets or some such—and was given a medal and what they call a battle-field commission. By all accounts he was a model soldier, both as an officer and an enlisted man. He never made trouble, was well thought of by those he commanded and those who commanded him. Not a blemish on his record. Which is why no one can understand this sudden change. The report we got stated that his commander thought of him as the last man to desert, under any kind of provocation."

"How long ago did they desert?"

Longarm reached over, took the bottle, and poured a little whiskey in his coffee. He said, "They were on patrol. Supposed to be out two weeks. But they never came back. So you could say they deserted when they left, which would be six weeks ago, or they deserted when they didn't come back. Which would make them deserters for a month. Only hitch to that theory is that Lieutenant Meadows was leading a seven-man patrol. Only six besides Meadows were seen at the bank. The seventh, a corporal name of Cupper, didn't show up."

"Do you think they would kill him? Their own comrade?"

He shook his head. "No, no, Molly, my darlin'. You are not going to get me to speculating about something I know nothing about. This was planned. There's no question about it. You'd of thought they'd have split up, put on civilian clothes, and disappeared. Instead they continue to wear their uniforms, and have gone into the bank-robbing business. At least they robbed *one* bank. But that uniform trick won't work again. It was effective the first time, but every bank in the surrounding territories and states has been notified. And they didn't get a great deal of money out of that San Angelo bank, not quite seven thousand dollars. Curious thing is that there's a cavalry post in San Angelo. Fort Concho. Took a little nerve."

Molly said, "That makes sense to me. Wouldn't they be accepted there in their uniforms and taken in as a matter of course?"

Longarm gave Molly a surprised look. He made a motion toward his shirt pocket, where he carried his badge when he wasn't wearing it. "Maybe you better put on this tin. That never occurred to me. And maybe that explains why they would make a one-hundred-fifty mile ride to San Angelo, passing other banks and towns on the way. Yes, by golly, I believe you are right. If that is the case, I think I had better take a look at the chain of forts across Texas, New Mexico, and Arizona. Maybe that's the way they plan to operate."

"You have no idea where they are now?"

He shook his head. "Trail is cold. And will be colder by the time I get down there. Personally, I think this is a wild-goose chance. My guess is they are going to try and hit enough banks, maybe two or three more, to get enough money to set every man up and then disband and disappear. I think they will have done that by the time I get cranked up and on the trail."

She put her hand on his forearm. "Longarm, I never told Mack his business and I'm not going to tell you yours. But this lieutenant doesn't sound like a man to be fooled with. I hope you are going to do as you say, find them and send for the cavalry, and not be so foolish as to try and apprehend them alone."

He looked at her as if to say, "Ok, Molly." Instead he said, "Lieutenant Meadows is puzzling in another respect. Just

11

before he left on that last patrol he applied to his commanding officer for permission to send for his fiancée and get married. Permission was granted, and they know he wrote the lady in question, a Miss Carol Ann Foster of Baltimore, Maryland—his home state by the way—proposing that she set out immediately and saying they would be married as soon as she arrived. The letter was seen by a fellow officer, and the company clerk posted it. Since then they have wired Miss Foster's home, and been informed that she left for Texas, in company with her younger sister, some two weeks past. Figuring the distance and some of the stretches she's had to go through, she ought to be just about to Fort Davis by now. Or damn close to it."

"*If* she was going to Fort Davis," Molly said dryly.

"What do you mean by that?"

"Suppose they had it made up all along that he'd desert and she'd meet him at some other place."

Longarm frowned. "A fellow officer of his read the letter. It seems that Lieutenant Meadows wasn't no great shakes with pen and ink, and he asked a more educated member of his tribe to look the letter over and make sure it was correct and done right. After all, it was an important letter."

"They could have had some kind of code. If I sign it one way meet me in Dallas, or if I start out with a particular word, that means to meet me in El Paso. Or Oklahoma City. All that could have been arranged in other letters beforehand."

Longarm rolled his eyes toward the ceiling. "I'm going to have to take your badge and deputy's commission back, Molly. You're sort of stretching it there."

"It could have happened."

"Why? The one has nothing to do with the other. If he was going to desert he could have done so and then sent for his girl. Why ask for permission to marry when deserters

12

don't need permission? And a code? Ah, Molly, I love your imagination in bed, but not as a deputy marshal. No, the girl has nothing to do with it except it's a cruel trick to play on her. That's a long hard journey to make only to find your prospective bridegroom has gone over the hill and is now a wanted criminal. All it tells me is that the desertion wasn't planned ahead of time. Something happened on that patrol to make those men desert. Something occurred that was of such a consequence they couldn't go back to the fort."

"You have any idea what it was?"

He shook his head. "So far nothing has turned up. But I'm going to trace their trail and see what I run across."

"Is there no way to reach the woman before she gets to her destination?"

Longarm shrugged. "I don't know what good it would do even if we could."

"You could at least find out if she knew of his plans. If you could find her maybe she'd lead you to him."

Longarm smiled. "That is, if she was privy to his plans to desert. You won't let go, will you, Molly."

"It wouldn't hurt to wire the railroad and have them be on the lookout for her."

Longarm sighed. "Molly, how many little one-track railroad companies can you name offhand out here in this part of the country? Hell, must be twenty-five or thirty. Some of 'em only go from one town to another. Which railroad you going to wire? The Missouri Pacific or the Southern Pacific or the Union Pacific? Those are mainline roads running from coast to coast. By now she's taken some little line has got mules pulling the cars. Hell, I'll be on at least four different lines getting to Fort Davis. Maybe more if I can't make connections."

She sighed, got up, got the big coffeepot off the stove, and poured his cup full.

He said, "Not so much. Leave me some room in there to add a little something."

"Like cream and sugar?"

"On occasion. This just don't happen to be one of those occasions." He took the whiskey bottle and added a shot to his black coffee. But the whiskey made the cup so full he had to bend over and slurp up a mouthful before he could lift the cup without spilling.

She said, "Well, it sounds as if you have a job of work cut out for you. I expect it will keep you out of trouble."

He yawned. He hadn't exactly gotten an uninterrupted night's sleep. He said, "We are just trying to give the impression we are cooperating. I figure it for a wild-goose chase. You got any idea how vast a country that is out there? They could head for New Mexico Territory or Arizona or down into old Mexico. Hell, they could even head north for Yankeeland. Who knows. I can't stop every man I see wearing a cavalry outfit. I'll play, but I ain't going to play hard. It might get down to they'll have to look me up if they want to be found."

She gave him a jaundiced look. "Custis, don't try that foolishness on me. You'll get your nose on their trail and you won't quit until you bring them in. Have you forgot who you are talking to? You and Mack weren't that much different. I've seen the look on both of your faces. You're like some old hound dog smelling squirrel."

He took out his watch. He said, "A squirrel ain't exactly the animal I got on my mind, but it does have a nice coat of red fur."

She stood up and put out her hand. "Then let's hurry so we don't have to hurry."

Chapter 2

It took him thirty hours and three train changes just to go across Oklahoma and duck south into Texas to Wichita Falls. He had not been exaggerating about the number of small lines that caused long waits and uncertainties of schedule as a traveler tried to make his way by railroad through the unsettled and nearly unsettleable areas of the north-central part of the Southwest. But he had known the difficulties when he'd chosen to go out of his way to spend some time with Molly. He didn't regret a moment of it, even when he was fretting through a six-hour delay just to catch a train that was only going to take him another hundred miles, of which only forty would be in the right direction.

He'd thought he'd be able to cut southwest out of Witchita Falls and head straight for Alpine, which was the nearest town to Fort Davis. But when he arrived that night, dusty and travel-worn, he discovered that his information was wrong. He'd have to go due west, right to the middle of the Texas panhandle, before he could cut south and then west toward his destination. That news finally made him cuss for a while, but then he hunted up a saloon in the dusty cattle town—

15

which seemed to have no reason for existing since, as far as Longarm was concerned, he hadn't seen enough grass to feed a calf, much less a herd. And it was July. If you didn't have grass in July, when could a man expect to have it?

But he had a couple of bar whiskeys, reflected he might as well have ridden cross-country horseback, and then went off to find himself a room for the night. He'd seen a poker game going in the saloon, and he figured to go back and join that later. He certainly had enough time. His train for Amarillo didn't leave until noon the next day. And the passenger agent, who was supposed to know such things, wasn't at all sure about a train south out of Amarillo on account of it being a competing line. He knew that one ran; he just didn't know the day or time.

Stumbling around in his dark hotel room, trying to find the kerosene lamp, and finding it, and then finding it was out of coal oil, he reflected that he didn't really much give a damn about all the difficulty. He intended to treat the whole assignment as a paid vacation, a time away from headquarters, Billy Vail, and the law business. Hell, he'd been in it long enough to get tired of it. So he was just going to meander down to Fort Davis, however and which-ever way the railroad tracks ran, and then meander over to San Angelo, and then, when enough time had passed, just meander on back to Colorado and tell whoever asked that he'd looked but he couldn't find any truant soldier boys. All he knew now was that the train to Amarillo took twelve hours. After that he was a solid six or seven hundred miles from Alpine, and he'd get there when he got there; mean-while he figured to notify the desk clerk that he needed a lamp in his room that actually made light, and then go over and play some poker. He hadn't had any supper and wasn't likely to get any, the hour being what it was, but maybe they'd have some crackers and cheese at the saloon.

16

The next day his luck started changing. He got into Amarillo at midnight, and found he could get a train out south the next morning that would take him to Lubbock and on to Odessa. That was better than halfway to Alpine. Schedules were uncertain after that, but it was a help. In the bigger town, even at the late hour, he was able to find a good supper, get a bath, get cleaned up and shaved, and get a good night's sleep. The next morning, in clean clothes and with a good breakfast in him, he swung aboard the departing train with the feeling he might actually accomplish something besides seeing how many miles of train travel he could survive.

By noon the next day the train was rattling across the flat, featureless plains of the Texas panhandle. Longarm looked out the window, seeing very little to recommend the country for human habitation. There was sage that would, in the last days of the summer, uproot itself and go tumbling across the prairie, running on the northwest wind, traveling tens and hundreds of miles to spread its seed in order to make more sage which was worthless to man and beast. There was greasewood and buffalo grass and small, stunted cedar brakes. That and sand. Longarm didn't reckon he'd ever seen so much powdery sand since the last time he'd been in the Texas panhandle. Now and again he'd see, through the open train window, the sagging remains of another failed sodbuster's attempt to build a house and barn, raise a crop, and feed a few milk cows and a wife and kids. Occasionally he'd see a man still struggling, busting up land to plant seed for corn or wheat or whatever it was that would dry out and die by September, now standing behind a plow horse and watching the train go by. And a couple of hundred yards further on, he'd see the man's wife and children in front of a house that had only been built a year before but was already starting to weather. They'd be standing there, the woman watching the train, shading her eyes with her hand, a small child clutching at each leg. Longarm just shook his head. As near as he could figure the only crop the country raised was dashed hopes.

He was riding the Texas and Rio Grande, a pretty fair line. As a federal marshal he could ride any line that the government did business with free of cost. In theory that worked pretty good, but often he found himself dealing with a ticket agent who had never heard of such an idea. So he found it an easier proposition just to lay out the two or three dollars, or whatever it was, and save the discussion. For that reason and others, his badge generally stayed where it was— in his shirt pocket. If he wore the badge while traveling, folks would stare at it, trying to figure out if he was a sheriff or a deputy or just what. Finally they'd ask, and that just meant answering a lot of fool questions. Besides, he'd been able to prevent more than one crime happening because the people about to make it happen didn't realize they had a federal marshal in their midst.

He rode, swaying with the rambling motion of the car. He'd bought some beef jerky at a grocery store, and he had that to eat along with a couple of apples. And his saddlebags were at his feet so he had a drink of whiskey handy in case the jerky made his mouth too dry.

The car was about half full. He'd noticed that the further toward the southwest he got, the shorter the trains got and the fewer passengers they carried. This one was a mixed train of five passenger coaches, a mail car, and what he guessed were about eighteen to twenty freight and cattle cars. His train was due in Odessa at five the next morning, and the ticket agent had assured him that he'd make connections with an express on the Texas and Rio Grande that would be coming through Odessa at six in the morning. If for some reason he missed that one, there was a local out no

18

more than half an hour later that would get him to Alpine. The agent hadn't known what line the local was on, but he'd assured Longarm that the T & RG didn't make connections with any but the most reliable lines.

Longarm privately thought that the agent was plenty long on assurances and not so sure about the actualities.

They got into Lubbock at a little after eight that night, about an hour behind schedule, but at least they were about halfway to Odessa. Longarm climbed down from the chair car and went into the depot to see if there might not be a nearby cafe where he could get something to eat to take along with him. He found a boy selling ham sandwiches wrapped in wax paper and jugs of apple cider out of a washtub filled with ice. He bought three sandwiches and a half-gallon jug of the cider, and sat down in the depot to eat and drink while sitting on something that didn't move around under him. But the motion of the train was still with him, and even sitting on one of the waiting-room chairs, he still felt like they were rattling along on the crooked rails at forty miles an hour.

He was about to get up and eat outside when his eye was caught by two women at the ticket agent's window. He judged them both to be in their mid to late twenties, though he thought the smaller of the two was the younger by several years. The taller was talking to the ticket agent and seemed agitated. Longarm watched. The taller woman was plain, but she would do in the dark, Longarm calculated, or for a man who didn't put too fine a point on looks. The smaller was wearing a bonnet—they both were—but Longarm could see wheat-colored curls peeking out from beneath the blue hat that was held in place with a ribbon under her chin. She was, he reckoned, a smaller copy of Molly, with the same hips and breasts except not quite as obvious. Both were wearing long skirts and tight bodices. The shirtwaist of the taller—

19

woman was like the panhandle prairie, flat except where it was relieved by two small humps. She did, however, have a certain flare to her hips that took Longarm's eye. But then they both did, except the shorter blonde's hips flared with more allure. Longarm couldn't quite see the blonde's face, and he was about to walk halfway across the room to where he could get a look at her, but just as he started to rise, she turned and he could see blue eyes, faintly rouged cheeks, and lips and a dainty face that were almost too pretty. He hoped they would be boarding his train. He was going to need something to look at through the monotony of the long night; the blonde would be just the thing.

While he was taking a drink of cider he heard the taller woman raise her voice to the ticket agent: "We have not come this far to be delayed again. I don't care what line my ticket is for. We have arrived from Dallas four hours ago, and I intend that we should make a connection out of Odessa and I will not stand for any more nonsense. Now whether you honor our tickets or not, I and my sister are boarding that train!"

Longarm listened and looked. They didn't appear to be sisters to his eye. But he was more taken with the woman's accent. She might have come *through* Dallas, but she sure as hell hadn't come *from* Dallas. He reckoned her accent to be from much further north, even though it had a sort of Southern quality to it, perhaps from Virginia. He had been to Virginia and had once, while on marshal business, had the occasion to spend the night in Washington, D.C., with a woman from Virginia. She sounded like his memory of that woman.

The women had two heavy suitcases with them and they both appeared travel worn and dusty. He figured, with a little brightening up, the blonde would be worth taking a closer look at. He tried, but couldn't see if either of them

20

was wearing a ring. He was sitting there trying to come to some conclusion about their background when the passenger agent apparently gave in. Longarm heard him say, "You're booked through Odessa to Alpine. Though I'll be blazed—pardon the language, ma'am—what difference it could make what line you git into Alpine. They're all of a piece and it ain't no question of money, more or less."

If the tall young woman replied Longarm didn't hear her. She turned away from the window and put her tickets into the small purse she was clutching in her hands. Longarm was interested now that he knew their destination was Alpine. There were two of them, and he was willing to bet that neither had a man waiting for her at their destination. And if either of them did, he hoped it was the taller, plainer woman.

The little blonde said so Longarm could hear, "Are you going to telegram now?"

"Oh, no, no. From Odessa. When we're sure."

Longarm wondered what they wanted to be sure about, but he was still trying to make up his mind about their quality. They were a long way from trash, but they weren't quite gentry. If he'd met them in the city, he would have guessed they were shop girls of some kind, or maybe they even worked in a bank. But this far west it was difficult to place them with his lawman's mind. Out here they would have certainly been the daughters of well-to-do ranchers or someone from the town gentry. But in the part of the country he was in, gentry meant you could read and write a little and maybe cipher some. When Billy Vail had first told him where he was headed, to the hardrock country of Texas, he'd said, "Oh, hell, Billy, I don't want to go back there. That is the dregs of the world. Hell, I ain't going to be able to find them anyway, so if I'm not, let me not find them in someplace a little more pleasant."

21

It was hard country, west Texas and eastern New Mexico. It was not only hard, but it was unsettled, rough, unkind, and even dangerous. The Comanches had been either dispersed or herded onto reservations, but the Apaches were still very much in business, and occupying the attention of a lot of the cavalry from the different forts. But even without the savages, it was a dangerous country, especially for two unprotected women who, if they weren't quality where they came from, stuck out like stars against a velvet black sky in such surroundings. And they were going even further into the interior of the hard rock country, going as far as he was. He wondered what business could be taking such fine-looking women—at least one fine-looking woman—to such a hellhole.

Billy Vail had answered his complaint with, "Well, Custis, as far as that goes I've seen you trying to eat peas with your fingers. Ought not be too quick to set yourself above others. You know the Good Book's attitude on that score."

He'd said, "Yes, Billy, but I am talking about folks that have never even seen a chair, much less actually sat in one. Hell, I don't want to go down to that ugly country and drink warm beer and eat bacon with the rind on it and try and get a woman to bed who needs a shave."

Billy Vail had just looked at him steadily and shook his head. Then he'd said, "You are getting soft, Custis. Was a day you would have considered them as treats and not hardships. Especially the woman with the mustache and hair under her arms. No, I can see now that I have let you stray from the pleasures of hard duty. So you are my man."

And now here were two ladies who very definitely were not hairy, especially the blonde.

The taller one said, "We had better get on the train." She looked around as if deciding which door to go out, and then bent to pick up her large valise.

But Longarm had been anticipating that moment ever since he'd heard that they were going his way. He'd laid his sandwich down with the others and put the cork back in the jug of cider and set it on the floor. So he was ready when the young woman started to pick up her valise. With two quick steps he was by their side. He said, "Let me help you ladies with them valises, please."

They both looked up at him, but it was the blonde who smiled. She said, "Why, yes, my gracious. How kind of you, sirh." He noted that the woman's "sir" wasn't quite Southern. It wasn't Yankee, but it wasn't Southern.

He picked up their luggage, a bag in each hand, surprised at their weight. He said, "Right this way, ladies. I reckon you are on the same train as I am. Heading south."

They followed him up the steps of the car and into the interior, which was well lit with kerosene lamps. At each end of the car were seats that faced each other. He said, "Ya'll care to sit here? You can each take a seat and have the whole thing to yourself. We'll be riding all night and you near 'bout have room to stretch out and maybe get a little sleep."

The younger one said, "Oh, I can't ride backwards, makes me sick."

The older said, "Oh, I don't mind."

So they settled themselves into the seats, facing each other, while Longarm wrestled their bags into the overhead rack. He was disappointed that the blonde was riding in the forward-facing seat. That meant, if he were to be able to look at her face, that he'd have to ride backwards in the seat opposite across the aisle. He didn't much care for riding backwards himself.

It was still a few minutes before the train was scheduled to pull out, though Longarm could feel the tremor through the coaches as the engineer kept the steam up in his boiler.

Longarm suddenly remembered his ham sandwiches and his jug of sweet cider. He said, "Pardon me a moment, ladies," and hurried off the train. His food and drink were still where he'd left them, and he decided to add to the lot in case the ladies cared for something. He bought two more sandwiches and another jug of apple cider, and got back on the train just as the bell started clanging and the conductor hollered out, "All aboard!"

Longarm got in his seat, sitting on the aisle part of the upright padded bench so he could better face the blonde, who also was sitting on the aisle side. The tall one was sitting next to the windows, back in the corner of her seat.

Longarm waited until the train had begun moving and settled into a rhythm before he offered the two women a ham sandwich and the new bottle of cider.

He said, "My name is Custis Long, ladies. I'm happy to make your accquaintance."

The blonde gave him a small smile and said, "How do you do, Mr. Long."

The tall one didn't say anything. Longarm held out the sandwiches. "I just bought these. I reckon they are fresh. And here's a jug of cider."

The blonde looked willing, but she turned her eyes toward the older woman. The plain one said, "No, thank you, Mr. Long."

Longarm had to turn his head all the way to the right to see her, and then he couldn't see her face clearly because she was back in the shadows. The car was well enough lit by the line of lamps down the center, but their glow didn't reach all the way to the corner by the window. Longarm said, "Well, how about a little cider if you ain't hungry. Could be a dry night. This country ain't famous for rain. They save water around here like poor folks save pennies. Have to drink their own bathwater if they want a wash."

The blonde almost laughed, or wanted to, but she looked over at the older girl again, who did not laugh. She might have been smiling, but Longarm couldn't tell.

"No, thank you," the older one said.

"It's sweet cider. A Baptist preacher's daughter could drink it."

"We're not thirsty."

Then the blonde surprised him. She said, "Well, I am. In fact I am parched. I wouldn't mind a drink of cider."

Longarm said, "I'll pull the cork for you."

Using his small pocketknife, he worked the cork up until he could get it with his front teeth and then drew it out. He tapped the cork back in lightly and then handed it across to the blonde. "Thank you," she said. "I am ever so much obliged."

Longarm said, "Just keep it right there with you. I got plenty." He held up his own jug. "And if you get to wanting a sandwich, why, sing out. I got plenty." Then he held up the bottle of whiskey he had in the seat beside him. "And if you care for something stronger, why, just sing out."

From the shadows the tall girl's serious voice said, "We don't hold with spirits, Mr. Long."

"I don't either as a general thing," he said. "But whiskey will work wonders for train sway." He looked at the blonde. "I hate to admit it but I suffer from the same curse as you. I tend to get a little sick on these land steam packets. But a touch of the old vinegar puts me right in no time."

He was aware that he was sounding folksy, and even softening his own crisp tones to fall more in line with theirs. He had traveled so much that he had almost no accent, but one of his talents had been his ability to put himself at home with whomever he was dealing with. He had learned, early, that words could sometimes be as effective as bullets. They were certainly a damn sight less final, he had often concluded. And of course, he didn't mind lying at all if he thought it would improve the situation. Lying, in his opinion, was an art often overlooked by the narrow-minded and shortsighted. It could be used to gain an advantage, it could be used to lay a false trail, delay, speed up, cancel, or persuade. He would have no more thought of traveling without a handy box of lies than he would have considered leaving his revolver at home. He had taken careful note that, while he had introduced himself, neither young lady had given her name. That too was a form of lying, though they might have considered it just the way to discourage the unwanted advances of a stranger. But the tall, plain sourpuss was much mistaken if she thought that he could be that easily put off in his stalking of the buxom little blonde.

With the train swaying and the good light and his advantageous position, he was able to more carefully consider the younger woman's breasts and he judged, by the way they seemed to want to fight their way out of her bodice, that they were more than ample, even by his standards. He loved small, thin-waisted girls with big breasts. They always seemed to come as such a nice surprise. A girl could be downright on the skinny side, and you'd be all set to be disappointed, and then the last of the top clothing would come off and out would come those beautiful, strawberry-tipped melons. It was better than Christmas, he judged, in the way of nice surprises.

Now that he had the older woman's opinion of liquor, he thought he'd better be discreet. He drank his cider down until the jug was only a third full, and then, turning to the side so that his body hid his work, he fed a liberal dose of whiskey in with the apple juice and then corked both bottles. He didn't give a hang for the plain girl's opinion of whiskey, but she seemed to hold some influence over the blonde one, so he determined it would be good politics to hang in her better graces. He doubted she had any really good ones, just varying degrees of less disagreeable graces.

But now that Longarm was comfortable with the fact that they were going to Alpine, which gave him plenty of time, he didn't mind the sourpuss riding herd. Of course it would help if he knew more about them and their business. The blonde stiffled a little yawn, and Longarm had the uneasy feeling he was going to lose her company early. He said, "Ya'll be traveling long?"

The blonde blinked her eyes and smiled just slightly. "Oh, my, yes. Quite a ways."

But she didn't ask about him, which would have only been polite. He said, "Must have come far."

"Oh, my, yes," she said.

He smiled to let her know he didn't mind her being close-mouthed. "Well, I know you are going to Odessa. Unless we have a train wreck."

A touch of real fright showed in her eyes. "Oh, don't say that! My brothers was teasing me about that same self thing before we left and they near scared me to death!"

Longarm could feel the eyes of the plain girl glowering at him out of the dark. But he said, "I most humbly beg your pardon. I bet they are little brothers. Little brothers can be a trial for a lady. My older sister shore can testify to that. Where are they?"

"Who?"

"Yore little brothers."

"Oh, they are at home. Are you what they call a cattle-man, Mr. Long?"

He considered. "Not in the strictest sense of the word. I have dabbled in cattle but they are not my main pleasure." He didn't say any more, figuring two could play at the game of concealment.

27

He waited, but she didn't inquire further, just sat there with her hands demurely folded in her lap, the jug of cider on the floor at her feet being kept from wandering from the sway of the train by her dainty shoe tips on each side.

Longarm got out a cigarillo. "You ladies mind if I smoke?"

He asked it in spite of the fact that, in the sparsely filled car, at least four other men were smoking and one of them was in the seat right behind the blonde.

The blonde didn't say anything, just gave a quick glance at her companion. Longarm wondered what she did when she had to go to the bathroom and the plain girl wasn't around to ask, did she just hold it?

The older girl said, "Please yourself."

"Thank you, ma'am," Longarm said. The flare of his match temporarily blinded him so that he didn't see the older girl shake her head in disapproval at the blonde. But if he'd seen it he wouldn't have been surprised. He'd come to think of the tall, prim girl as like most of the schoolteachers he'd known in his learning years. Their message was generally that if a thing is pleasant or fun or tastes good or smells good or has any good about it, you can be sure it is bad. To his eye they had all had the same unsmiling, uncomfortable, disapproving look about their mouth as this one did.

Well, he was a man who'd laid siege to a cabin full of bandits and waited a week for them to try something foolish. And that had been in the middle of the Arizona desert with no shade and little water and not much food to see him through. He reckoned he could wait in the relative comfort of a railroad passenger car until the train got to Alpine and he could get a chance to cut the blonde off from her traveling companion.

A few times it had idly entered his mind that the blonde could be the fiancée that the deserter, Lieutenant Meadows,

28

had sent for, but he judged that to be too big of a coincidence. Besides, she looked mighty young to have struck a match with a man who'd spent most of six years soldiering in Indian country. When would they have had a chance to court? By letter? By telegram? The girl was too young to have known him romantically before he'd left for the West. Likely she was the daughter of some big rancher around Alpine who'd been sent East to school some years back. For all he knew the prim sourpuss might actually have been one of her tutors at whatever girls school she'd been attending. Maybe they were heading to the blonde's home for a vacation from school. It was July and maybe the blonde had told so many stories about ranch life in the middle of the Big Lonesome that the tutor had come along to catch her in her lies. If that was the case, Longarm reflected, Miss Sourpuss was in for the shock of her life. No matter how the blonde might have stretched the hardships of such a life, the tutor would quickly find that the reality was worse than the fiction.

But then Longarm remembered she'd said her little brothers had been teasing her about train wrecks. Well, maybe they were at school too. Certainly, if a man was to get his children any sort of education, he had to send them out of that deep west Texas country. The only education there was based on first staying alive and second figuring out how to wring a living out of the unforgiving land and climate.

No. She had said they were at home. And she had never said where home was. The two travelers were either runaways, Longarm reckoned, or the closest-mouthed pair of women he'd ever had the misfortune to run across.

The miles ran on and the time got later. Longarm could feel his eyelids growing heavy when he heard a quiet voice from the shadows say to the blonde, "Janice, why don't you stretch out as best you can and try and take a little sleep.

Use your jacket for a pillow. Should be room for you."

The blonde yawned and nodded. "I just think I will."

So at least he knew her name was Janice. That was a start. Maybe if they traveled together for a week he might learn the first initial of the other one's first name.

Just as Janice settled herself around to stretch out on the hard seat the conductor came through trimming down the overhead lamps. He walked with the sure step of the land sailor he was, stepping easily to the sway of the coach. By the time he got to the end the coach was dim so that Longarm could no longer see the form of Janice clearly. He stopped the conductor as he passed and asked the time since he hadn't thought to look at his watch earlier. The conductor said, "Goin' on fer 'leven o'clock, neighbor. We got a long night of it."

"We close to on time? I got a connection out of Odessa."

The conductor said, "Ain't no way to know about a schedule out here, mister. Ain't no landmarks in the dark an' we don't make no stops. An' ever'body's got a connection at Odessa 'cause that's as fer as this here train goes."

After the conductor was gone Longarm had a few pulls from his doctored-up apple cider, and then leaned back in the corner his seat made with the coach wall. It was going to be a long ride and he might as well get as much sleep as he could. With his eyes adjusted to the dimness, he could make out the form of the older girl sitting primly upright and staring out the window at the darker night that was outside. Not a light showed anywhere to give a sign that there were any other people alive beyond the glass of the window.

Longarm smoked one last cigar while he stared at the prim young woman and wondered who she was and who she thought she was and where in hell was she going. He'd seen several other women on the train, but they'd looked

30

at home in the country they were traveling in. They were older women, rougher women, women who looked a great deal more like they belonged than the pair who were his neighbors.

But Longarm was not a man to speculate on a mystery that didn't concern him. Likely, he thought, it would have some simple explanation by the time they reached their common goal in Alpine.

He came awake suddenly to the echoing sound of the door being slammed at the far end of the car. Automatically he sat up, his senses alert. At the far end the conductor was making his way forward, trimming up the wicks of the overhead lamps. It was solid dark outside the train window, but the car was gradually coming to life and light as the conductor made his way forward. He called out in a bored voice, "Next stop, Odessa. All out at Odessaaa. Connections for south, east, and westbound trains. Odessa, next stop, twenty minutes!"

The two women were just sitting up and yawning as the conductor got to them. He consulted a clutch of tickets in his hand and said, "You ladies will be changing in Odessa for Alpine. You'd best rustle right along. Yore train will be settin' in the depot with steam up."

Longarm couldn't see her, but he could hear the taller woman when she said, "I have to send an important telegram. Will I have time?"

The conductor said, "I wouldn't make no day's work out of it, ma'am. That southbound train is rarin' to go. Only waitin' on us."

Longarm heard Janice say, "Don't worry about the bags. I'll get them. You run straight for the telegrapher's."

When the conductor was gone Longarm reached up to his overhead rack and took down his saddlebags and his Model 1873 Winchester lever-action carbine. He set them in his

31

seat next to the window, and then reached for the bags of the two young women. He set them sideways in the aisle so people could still pass. He said to the blonde, "I'm on that Alpine train. Ya'll tend to your business and I'll see your bags safely aboard."

The tall one gave him a look. He could see her clearly now that he was standing. She said, "That won't be necessary."

He looked at his watch. It was ten minutes to five in the morning. It would be dark another hour, if not a little more. He said, "Don't mind, miss. Your bags are pretty heavy."

He could see Janice giving her companion a look. The tall one shrugged. She said, "You go with him, Janice. If you can, get us the same seats. It's still a long ride and we want to be as comfortable as possible."

The tall one didn't look at Longarm, but Janice flashed him a smile of pure gold. "That would be ever so nice of you, Mr. Long. The bags *are* heavy."

The tall one said, as if fearful of leaving Janice to Longarm's clutches, "I'll be as quick as I can, Janice. It shouldn't take more than five minutes."

"I'll be fine," Janice said. She cut her eyes at Longarm. "I'm sure Mister Long will look after me."

"Yes," the tall one said dryly.

Longarm sat back down as he began to feel the train slow. He resented the plain girl's attitude. Hell, he had just gotten out of the bed of a woman who would make four of her and two of the blonde. And by rights, he should feel guilty about the way he was building his next bed so soon after Molly. But he didn't because Molly was an old hand, just like himself, and she would understand that he had to take any opportunity that might present itself, heading into barren territory as he was. He had considered it the most inconceivable stroke of good luck that the two women were going to a place where women were scarce enough to command almost any price. Molly wouldn't blame him for having a look at the cards in his hand, and he reckoned she would damn sure resent the sourpuss's attitude that he was up to anything more than a healthy male's interest in a pretty girl.

The train was slowing more and more. Pretty soon the bell would begin to toll, and then would come the whistle as it blew for the station, and then the slowly increasing sound of steel on steel, squealing as the engineer put on the brakes.

In the car other passengers were starting to their feet, getting their luggage down and collecting their baggage. Janice said, "You'd better get right at the door."

"Yes," the tall one said. "I will."

She got up and went through the car door into the vestibule that led to the outside.

When she was gone Longarm said, "Alpine is a hell of a place for a couple of ladies like yourselves."

"Is it?" Janice said.

"I take it ya'll are sisters." He had heard the tall one say they were.

"No," Janice said. "We're not sisters."

As the train began to lurch to a stop Longarm stood up and put his saddlebags over his shoulder. He would take each of their bags in a hand. But that left his carbine. He said to Janice, "Do you reckon you could carry my rifle?"

"Oh, yes."

"Won't scare you?"

"Oh, no."

He handed it to her and bent to pick up their valises. As he straightened up with the load he wondered, as close-mouthed as the pair were, whether they'd trained as nuns, taking a vow of silence. It would be just his luck if they had, especially the blonde.

33

Chapter 3

Even in the dark Longarm was disappointed by the sight of their new train. In the glow of the lights from the depot he could see the small, dinky engine. It was what was called a donkey engine, the kind the big lines used to switch cars around in their freight yards. That meant the trip was going to be slow, slower still if they had any grades to climb, and it was also an indication that any line that used such an engine for the three-hundred mile haul to Alpine was not doing as well as it might. He also took note of the short smokestack. That meant that they would have to keep the windows closed to keep the cars from filling up with smoke and sparks and cinders. It was, he reckoned, going to be a long, uncomfortable ride.

He couldn't see how many cars the train was comprised of since it disappeared into darkness, but he couldn't reckon it was too many. He steered Janice to the door of the first car and, ladened as he was with valises and saddlebags, still managed to give her a hand up the steps. She carried his rifle all wrong, with the barrel pointing in first one direction and then the next, but that didn't matter because there was no shell in the chamber. She'd also brought along his sandwiches and her jug of cider. His cider and whiskey jug along with his bottle of whiskey were in his saddlebags.

He got inside and was relieved to discover that the car, though shorter than the car of the train they'd just left, was set up in practically the same manner. He'd seen the name of the line on the coal tender. It was something called the Odessa West & El Paso. He'd smiled a little. A run from Odessa to El Paso via Alpine was better than four hundred miles and he could just imagine such an engine making it that far. As it was, he figured they'd have to stop every fifty miles for the engine to take on water on account of the size of its boiler.

He got Janice settled, got their valises overhead, and then stored his own gear, being sure the whiskey bottle was in reach along with his diluted jug of cider.

When they were both seated he said, "Reckon your friend there is telegraphing Alpine to let them know ya'll are on your way and that you made your train."

She said, "I guess." Then she got up. "I expect I'd better look for her. She might not see the train straightaway."

Longarm laughed. "Only one here except the one she just got off of and they are turning that one around."

But she got up without listening and went through the door and out into the vestibule. He looked at his watch in the dim glow of the overhead lamps. The light was not as good as on the other car, but he could make out that it was close on to five-thirty. He reckoned they'd be pulling out any minute. He put his watch away and had a good long pull of cider and whiskey as substitutes for both breakfast and coffee. He'd eat a sandwich after they got going good, and maybe by then the ladies wouldn't be too proud to share with him. They were, he reckoned, the hardest-to-get-to-know pair of fillies he'd ever run across. He wondered if he was getting too old or if he'd lost his touch or if they were just plain

35

not interested. He contented himself with the thought that they might well have taken religious vows and were no longer interested in matters of the flesh. He wondered if the clenched-faced one ever had been. It amused Longarm to think she probably envisioned every man as desperately seeking to possess her body, and not only to possess it, but to root around in her and ravish her. The thought almost made him laugh out loud. He'd known a few old maids that had carried such a conviction to their graves, not ever noticing that they'd gone their whole lives without even getting their hair mussed.

He was still faintly smiling when the prim one got back on the train. Janice asked her anxiously if she'd gotten the telegram off.

"Just barely," she said, the disapproval heavy in her voice. "I swear, I cannot begin to imagine how they are going to settle this country with the level of competence as it is around here. The man was an idiot. And half asleep. And half drunk, I wouldn't be surprised."

"But you did get it off?"

"Oh, yes."

Longarm watched Janice as she smoothed her skirt. She said, "Well, now, then it is out of our hands. All we have to do is enjoy the train ride and wait for what happens."

Longarm thought she must have lead a sheltered life if she was planning to enjoy the ride, but he didn't say anything. His mind was busy wondering what she had meant when she'd said "wait for what happens." It was an odd remark to make. Though maybe she was talking about some misfortune like a train wreck. Well, he doubted that this short-coupled donkey train was likely to get up enough speed to have much of a wreck.

The tall girl was looking around. She said, "This seems a much smaller coach than the one we were on."

Longarm said, "It is."

But the tall woman ignored him. She said to Janice, "I guess we'll do without breakfast. I certainly thought we'd have more time at the depot than we did."

Longarm said, "Maybe ya'll would fancy them sandwiches now." He took two off the seat beside him and handed them across the aisle. "Might be a little older than they was last night, but I doubt they've grown whiskers."

Janice started to put out her hand to take one, but then looked at the older woman. The tall girl was eyeing the sandwich in Longarm's right hand but she made no attempt to take it. Finally she said primly, "We wouldn't want to deprive you. It's a long ride."

"I got plenty," Longarm said. "I can promise you it's all the food you are going to see between here and Alpine." He was starting to get just a touch irritated. He didn't know who the hell the tall bitch thought she was, but he was getting tired of hanging his arms across the aisle. He said, "Better make up your mind before my arms drop off."

The pinched-face woman sighed. She put out a hand and took the sandwich and said, as if she was conferring a favor, "Oh, very well. Though I hate to accept hospitality I can't return."

Janice grabbed hers and said gratefully, "Thank you very much, Mr. Long. I am ever so hungry." Then she put her hand out to her companion and said, "And we even have cider to drink with it. I brought the jug from the other train. Mr. Long's hands were quite full with our bags and his saddle affair. I can't recall what he called it."

"Saddlebags," Longarm said. "You carry them behind you on a horse. You ladies must be city dwellers. I didn't reckon was anybody didn't know a pair of saddlebags when they saw them."

They both nodded at him and gave their own versions of a smile, though Longarm was hard pressed to recognize the sourpuss's as such.

Then, for a little while, no one spoke as all three ate. Longarm finished first, and then dusted the bread crumbs off his hands and wadded up his sandwich wrapper. He said conversationally, feeling now that he'd fed them they ought to be more agreeable to talk, "So ya'll are going to Alpine?"

Janice nodded, chewing. After a moment she said, "Yes."

"Mind if I ask whatever for? Place don't seem to suit two high-style ladies such as yourselves. Ever'body there knows what a pair of saddlebags are."

They made no answer. Longarm might have put it down to their interest in their food, but he doubted it. For some reason these two ladies didn't seem much inclined to talk. If he'd been just another man, he'd have quickly figured they were politely handing him his hat and making it clear he didn't appeal. But he was a lawman, and he had a streak of curiousity and inquisitiveness and suspicion that came with the badge. The women might not care to talk, but he was determined that they should.

Outside the window the inky night was starting to give way to a faint glow of dawn. By his watch it was almost half past six. Even as he watched, the sky turned rosy, and then little streaks of clouds could be seen against the morning sky. They were high up, he knew, and would never bring one drop of rain to the barren country. But the light of day was welcome. He felt as if he'd been traveling through the night for weeks.

He was watching the sunrise through the window across the car that was between the seats of the two women. The train was headed south so east was on their side. He heard the older one say to Janice, "Thank heavens, it's finally daylight. Maybe we'll go around a curve and I can have a look at this train. I noticed we were the first car behind the coal tender. I'm not sure that's usual. I thought the baggage car or the mail car would come before the passenger coaches."

Longarm said, thrusting his voice in again, "I wouldn't count on this being much of a train, miss. I got a look at that engine and it ain't big enough to pull much more than itself, and that downhill."

The older one turned her head and looked at him. Now that the car was flooding with sunlight he could see that she was older than he had thought. He reckoned her to be pushing thirty. Always before, he'd seen her in the soft light of kerosene lamps, and that was deceptive. She said, "What do you mean, small engine? Aren't they all the same?"

He shook his head. "No. If you got a short cargo, what would you want with one of them big locomotives like they have on the main line? I doubt this train is pulling more than three or four cars, and one of them is going to be a caboose."

She got a slightly alarmed look on her face. "Are you saying they might not have a mail car?"

The question puzzled him, but he figured she had a reason for asking it. He said, "If they got a government contract to haul mail, yes, it will have a mail car. But they ain't going to let you ride in it if that was your idea. Them employees in there is special. Government and bonded. Car's kept locked. Don't let ordinary folks in."

She gave Janice an alarmed look. Then she said, "But they have to have a mail car. This is the train for Alpine!"

Longarm said, "Yeah, but it ain't the only train for Alpine. There is two lines run over this road. One is part of that train we got off in Odessa, the Texas & Rio Grande. It goes to Alpine as well. But this here train is the Odessa West & El Paso. Though I ain't real sure about that El Paso part. I reckon that is just wistful thinking on the part of the board of directors of this outfit."

Now trouble was all over her face. She was staring at her companion but she was speaking to Longarm. "How could this have happened? We have tickets! Tickets on the Texas & Rio Grande. I made that utterly clear to that idiot back in that horrid town. What was its name?"

"Lubbock," Longarm said helpfully.

"I told him specifically. I argued with him that he make sure."

Longarm had been leaning back against the V his seat made with the coach wall. But now he sat up straight. "Miss, I overheard that conversation. I think the agent thought you was concerned about having to pay for another ticket. So did I. He took it you just wanted to get to Alpine. He was trying to reassure you that you'd make a train to Alpine this morning. He just didn't say which one."

Her face twisted in agony. "Oh, my God!"

Janice put out her hand to her. "Carol, you don't know for sure. Don't get upset. Please."

The name went off like a bell in his head. The name Carol, or even Carol Ann, might be fairly common, but he wondered, being the gambler that he was, what would be the odds on a woman with that name heading for Alpine and Fort Davis and maybe a marriage to a deserter who wasn't going to be there. He couldn't remember her last name now—it was scribbled down somewhere in the papers in his saddlebags—but the first thing he'd noticed about the two women had been their accents, which he'd placed as from near Virginia. The deserter, Meadows, was from Maryland, as was his fiancée, and that was near Virginia, and Washington, D.C., for that matter. Both their accents

40

were the same as he'd remembered from his several trips to the nation's capital.

He wasn't going to tell her, but he reckoned he was traveling in the company of a woman who was heading for a very great disappointment.

But what he couldn't figure out was her interest in the mail car and being sure that she was on the Texas & Rio Grande line. What in hell did all that mean?

He got no further in his thinking because she was saying to him, "Mr. Long, if you will pardon me . . ."

He leaned forward. "Yes, ma'am? What can I do for you?"

She was greatly agitated. "How can I make sure I'm on the right train? I need to know if there is a mail car on this train."

He said, looking out the window and seeing the smoke from the short smokestack blowing almost down to passenger level, "Well, if it wasn't for the smoke you could open a window and look back. But I don't recommend that. Best bet I reckon is to get ahold of the conductor and ask him."

"Where would he be?"

"Back in the caboose most likely. But he'll be coming forward once he's had his coffee or his breakfast to take up tickets. Until then I don't rightly know what you can do. Is it so important that you be on a train with a mail car?"

He couldn't be sure, but she looked as if she were about to cry. Her face was knotting up and she was clenching her fists. She said, "The damn stupid railroads! How could it have gotten so confused!"

He knew the answer to that one because the agent in Amarillo had explained it. He said, "There's two trains out of Odessa at nearly the same time. One is the through train from Austin and the other one is this one. For a destination like Alpine, that ain't as well served as some other points,

41

most folks just take the first one that's handy. It appears to me that we got in early on that run out of Lubbock where ya'll boarded and we beat the Austin train in there. I reckon they figured we didn't want to wait so they just loaded us aboard and sent us on our way. Or that Austin train might have been delayed. You don't want to plan a party counting on these little lines down here to fetch yore guests on time. You'll more than likely end up eating birthday cake by yourself."

He had meant it to console her, but it didn't seem to have any effect. She stared at Janice and said dully, "What am I to do?"

"You did send the telegram?"

"Oh, yes. It's too late for that." She looked miserable.

Janice said, "Maybe we'll stop at another town and you can send a new wire." She looked at Longarm.

Longarm shook his head. "Only place of any real habitation between here and Alpine, or Fort Davis, whichever you want to call it, is Fort Stockton, and we go thirty or forty miles west of it. Country was too rough to route the rails through Fort Stockton, even though the soldiers from that fort was the main protection for the workers while this line was being laid."

"Yes," the one named Carol said, "I know about Fort Stockton. I know we don't go there."

He said, "I still don't understand what difference the train makes. If you are meeting someone they'll expect the train to be early or late anywhere from one to five or six hours. Folks around here are used to it."

She slumped back in her seat and folded her hands in her lap. "It doesn't matter."

Janice leaned forward and put her hand on her friend's knee. "Carol, don't despair. Wait for the conductor. We still may be on the right train."

Carol sighed. "No. I know in my heart that I have made a mistake. The mistake of my life."

"I reckon I'm being a shade on the nosy side," Longarm said. "But it is my ambition to know what is so important about a mail car being on this train."

Carol was still slumped back in her chair. Without looking at Longarm she said, "Nothing. Really, it doesn't matter." But Longarm noted that that wasn't what her face was saying. He had never thought her pretty, even in the poor light of the depot the night before. But she'd had something about her, an authority, a presence that had made her attractive in a plain sort of way. But now, with her face puddled in misery, there was nothing fetching about her at all.

Janice said to him, "Carol Ann doesn't want to talk right now, Mister Long, if you don't mind."

"Not at all," he said. "I just wanted to help anyway I could. I hate to see a body just all unhappy that way." He sat back against the thin cushions of his seat thinking, well, that about clinches it. With a Carol Ann going to Alpine supposedly to meet a fiancé, this had to be the same one. He wouldn't bet a red cent on the girl being anyone else. For a few minutes he racked his brain trying to think of her name.

Foster. Carol Ann Foster.

Well, if Carol Ann Foster thought she was unhappy now, she need only wait a while to find out what unhappy really was. She'd ridden a train all the way from Maryland only to find out her fiancé had deserted the cavalry on just about the same day she'd left to meet him. And she was arriving on the wrong train. Longarm reckoned that this was not the woman he wanted standing behind him for luck when he was playing poker. She was black-catted and no mistake.

But he still wondered what in hell the mail car, or lack of one, had to do with things.

Janice had moved over and was sitting by her companion with her arm around her trying to console the miserable woman. Carol Ann hadn't openly wept yet, but Longarm figured it was only going to take final confirmation from the conductor to accomplish the job.

But he didn't know what the damn woman was getting so distraught about. For all she knew the train might have a mail car on it.

Though he doubted it. Over any given route the government only awarded one mail contract, and that usually went to the biggest outfit, and he greatly doubted that the Odessa West & El Paso was the king of the iron rails in that part of Texas.

He looked out the window. The country was still rolling plains, parched and dry, but in the far distance he could see faint outlines of hills and ridges and small mountains. Within a hundred miles the country would begin to roughen up, and where it had just been harsh and flat it would now be harsh and jagged.

It was not quite eight o'clock when the conductor put in an appearance at the rear of their car. He came slowly forward, stopping to take tickets from the few other people in the coach. Longarm watched Carol Ann come erect in her seat, her eyes riveted on the man in the blue suit with the funny little hat. He had a little punch in his hand, and he would take the ticket from a passenger, punch a hole in it, and then hand it back as a receipt to show the passenger had paid. But Longarm was far more interested in watching the two women. Janice glanced backwards, watching the conductor's progress. Carol Ann was leaning forward, eager to speed his arrival.

He stopped two seats from Longarm and punched the ticket of a man who looked like he belonged to the country. Longarm had his ticket out as the conductor came to his side.

44

He punched a hole in the strip of cardboard and then handed it back, glancing at Longarm over his rimless eyeglasses. He said, "This is a hell of a country to be paying money to go through, ain't it."

"Yeah," Longarm said, "but I don't reckon I got to look at it as much as you do."

"I reckon you are right," the conductor said. Longarm judged him a man in his late fifties. He looked like not much surprised him. He turned to the two women. "How be you ladies this fine morning? Need your tickets. Pretty as ya'll are, you might have slipped aboard and didn't reckon I'd care. But I fooled you. I'm too old to let beauty get away with a free ride. Only reason the railroad keeps me on the payroll."

Longarm could almost hear them holding their breaths while the conductor was punching their tickets. His view of Janice was partly blocked by the conductor, but he could see Carol Ann plainly. She was looking eagerly up into his face. She said, "Sir, oh, sir. Please, I need to know something."

"Yes, ma'am. I'll tell you anything except whether I'm married or not."

But Carol Ann was not in the mood for his tired jokes. She said, an edge in her voice, "Is there a mail car on this train?"

Longarm couldn't see the conductor's face, but he imagined he blinked and looked surprised. He said, "A what? A mail car?"

"Yes, a mail car." Her face was anxious. Longarm could see her twisting her fingers in her lap.

The conductor said slowly, "Well, no, ma'am, ain't no mail car, but it wouldn't have done you no good. If you was wantin' to mail a letter they don't do that on mail cars on railroads. See, they just transport the mail. You got a letter you'll just have to wait till Alpine. Maybe you was

45

wantin' to buy a stamp. I ain't right sure, but I might have a stamp or two back there in the caboose."

"No, no, no!" she said, and Longarm could hear the anguish in her voice, almost hear the tears. "There was supposed to be a mail car on this train! What has become of it? I'm on the wrong train! How did this happen? How *could* it have happened!"

Longarm saw the conductor reach up a hand and scratch the back of his neck. He reckoned the man was as mystified as *he* was. The conductor said slowly, "Ma'am, I don't know about you being on the wrong train. Yore ticket says Alpine and that is where we be headed. We'll get there. We might have to stop for water more than the through train, but we'll get you to Alpine. I don't know what a mail car has got to do with it, but it don't say no place on yore ticket that we got to get you to Alpine on no mail car train."

She lifted her hands and let them fall back in her lap. Her voice rose and fell in the same appeal. "But what *happened* to it? How did I miss it?"

Longarm would have liked to have seen the conductor's face, but he imagined it was as perplexed as *he* felt. The conductor said, "Well, they is two trains to Alpine 'bout the same time. That's us and the Texas and Rio Grande. The T&RG has got the mail contract so I reckon they are hauling the mail car. Not that I see what difference it makes. They are a faster train, but they ain't no more than two or three hours different."

Carol Ann gave a loud sigh and flopped back against the seat rest. She said, "Oh, hell! Damn! I am finished."

Longarm didn't know about the conductor, but he was surprised to hear such language come out of such a prim-looking lady. But before anyone could say anything Janice said, "But how could it have happened? We had tickets on that other train, the mail train."

The conductor shrugged and looked around at Longarm as if seeking help. Then he took a step down the aisle toward where he'd come and turned so he was facing all three. Carol Ann was lying back in her seat with her eyes closed. Janice was sitting on the edge of hers, turned so she could see the conductor. The conductor stood there, leaning an arm on each row of aisle seats. He said, "Well, ma'am, I don't know as the question has ever come up before, but I reckon the way it worked out was the through train from Austin come through early. He picked up them passengers that was there waiting and then went on knowing that we, this here train, was settin' there waiting to make connections with the train coming down from Lubbock. Normally he comes in behind us, but I reckon he didn't have to make some stops he normally does. Business been off a little here lately." He pointed behind him down the car. "You can see we ain't nowheres near as full as we ought to be. I reckon that's what happened. He's usually an hour behind us. But he got in a half hour before we was scheduled to leave, and you know ain't no express gonna wait around and let a little hoot-and-whistle outfit like us get on the track in front of him. We'd of slowed him up all to hell. I reckon he's a good hour, hour and a half ahead of us right now."

Janice said, her face showing the strain, "But how can that be? We were *told* we were taking that train. The agent *promised* us. It was on the timetable."

The conductor shrugged. He said, "I'm right sorry, miss, though I still don't know what all the fuss is about. As a general rule you don't want to put a lot of stock in railroad timetables or schedules when you get down in this part of the country. They ain't exactly all that dependable. We just mainly try and get folks where they be going the best way we can. I reckon it ain't as organized as it is up there in the East or the North, but we generally get the job done.

47

I don't know what this mail car business is all about, but we'll get you to Alpine if the boiler don't blow up."

Janice said, "But you don't understand. We sent a telegram! We wired ahead."

The conductor nodded. A look of understanding broke on his face. "I see," he said. "Ya'll wired you'd be on the express. That's the one with the mail car, the one out of Austin. Though I'm blamed for a fool if I know how you knowed about the mail car being on the T&RG. You've wired to folks meeting you and they will be expecting you on that through train." He nodded again. "Now it makes sense. But don't worry your pretty little heads. Folks you got meetin' you won't be too surprised. If they been in this country a while they'll understand and look for you comin' in next. Happens all the time. We'll be about three hours behind that other train, but we'll still make our schedule. By the time we get there that T&RG will nearly already be to the Mexican border."

Carol Ann sighed again, and Janice just nodded at the conductor and sat back around in her seat. The conductor said cheerfully, "Well, ya'll enjoy the ride an' holler if I can he'p you."

Longarm watched him leave the coach, and then he looked over at the two women. Carol Ann was staring at the ceiling and Janice was looking intently at her companion. Janice said, "It will be all right, Carol. It will be all right."

Carol Ann left off her study of the ceiling long enough to flick her eyes at her friend. "Don't be silly, Janice. It's over. And all because of a stupid mistake by the idiotic railroad company." She put her hand against the wall of the coach as if for support. "I can't believe it. After all this time, all our plans. And to have them ruined by a stupid mistake on a timetable. No. It wasn't stupid. It was criminally careless. One train is the same as another. Oh, God!"

She looked as if she were going to cry. Longarm was itching to question her, but he judged the timing was not exactly right. But something about the whole situation did not feel right to him. Something was making the short hairs at the back of his neck prickle. Something was dead wrong and it had to do with more than just a train schedule. Whatever it was had devastated one of the women and given the other a hard frown and worried eyes.

Janice said, "He'll understand."

Carol raised her head off the back of the seat and stared at her friend. "Him? Janice, have you taken leave of your senses? I'm as good as dead. You know him. He doesn't forgive."

Longarm could only conclude she was talking about her fiancé and that he wouldn't forgive her being late. But that didn't make a damn bit of sense. You didn't wait years for a woman and then throw her away because she got on the wrong train and was three hours late.

Janice said, "All right, he'll be angry. Very angry. But there will be other opportunities, other chances. We, you, will just have to convince him that something else can be arranged. Hope he will understand."

Carol Ann just put her head back against the seat and shook it slowly from side to side. "Think of something else. That's out."

"Is there anyplace we can leave the train?"

"They say it doesn't stop."

"Maybe we could get off anyway. Near some ranch or something."

Carol Ann pointed toward the window. "In that? Look at it."

Even as she finished speaking Longarm felt the train starting to slow. Janice said, alarm in her voice, "What's happening? Why are we slowing down? Are we going to stop?"

Longarm swiveled around and looked out the window. "I'd reckon it's a water stop. This little engine takes a power of water to keep chugging." He looked at his watch. They were a little better than three hours out of Lubbock. He figured they couldn't have come much more than a hundred miles, not at the speed the little locomotive was capable of. He didn't reckon they'd ever gotten much over thirty-five miles an hour.

As they slowed the curtain of smoke lifted and thinned. Longarm judged it was safe to raise a window without filling the car with smoke. He worked the window up two feet and cautiously stuck his head out, squinting his eyes to protect them from blowing embers. Ahead, about a half a mile, he could see a big water tank sticking up on the desolate plain. It looked odd, out of place in the barren, uninhabitable country. He pulled his head back in and shut the window. "Yep," he said, "water stop. He'll pull off the line on to a siding and fill up his boiler. Won't be long."

Janice said tensely, "Is there anyone there? Did you see anyone?"

Longarm shook his head. "A water tank ain't manned. The train crew handles the work. All they got to do is swing the long spout out and pull open a valve and let her pour. Ain't that much to it."

But her face was still tense. She said, "Are you sure nobody was there?"

He looked at her curiously. "Was you expecting someone? A water tank out in the big middle of nowhere ain't exactly a meeting hall."

She sat back. "No. I was just curious."

"Be a good chance to stretch your legs. Though if the wind is blowing you can get dusty faster than you can wash it off. This west Texas dust is like powder. It's dried-out

50

caliche clay that the wind sort of blows up and grinds down. It's as fine as light bread flour."

The car began to shudder as the faint squeal of the brakes throwing steel against steel sounded. There were bumps as the slack was taken up in the couplings between cars.

Longarm stood up. "I reckon I'll get me a dose of fresh air. These cars get a little stuffy with all the windows shut."

He walked to the door, opened it, and stepped through into the vestibule between cars. The exit door was of the Dutch variety and the top half had been swung back and fastened. Longarm leaned out and watched as the water tank slowly approached. It was like a huge, wooden barrel with a long spout, maybe twelve feet long, that swung out over the tracks. The train was already on the siding and coming to a stop with big puffs of steam. It didn't bother blowing its whistle or ringing its bell because there was no one to hear it except jackrabbits, gophers, snakes, and scorpions. Slowly it came to a stop, and then sighed and seemed to almost sag backwards. Longarm opened the bottom half of the door and took the long step down to the ground. He looked around. It was cooler and the air had a different feel. He knew that was because they were on a high plain, maybe at five thousand feet, that was called the *llano estacado*, the "staked plains." He'd never know why it was called that, but it described a high shelf of land that began in deep west Texas and ran west for a couple of hundred miles into New Mexico Territory. It was arid, barren, and fierce in summer heat or winter cold. But now, in early July, it was very pleasant. He stood there, looking around, watching the train crew swinging the spout around to fill the boiler with water. With the engine just making little chuffing sounds it seemed very quiet. He walked off a little ways to lean against a lone scrub oak, light a cigarillo, and watch the proceedings around the water tank. Out of the corner of his eye he saw the two women getting down from the train. They were a wonder and a mystery and no mistake. It could turn out to be nothing, but he was damned if he'd ever heard such a to-do made about whether a train had a mail car on it or not.

He glanced their way. They were standing a few feet from the train and the other passengers who'd gotten off, talking earnestly. Or at least Janice was talking. The other one, Carol Ann, looked too dazed to seem to do much more than listen. Longarm thought that he would give a crystal pistol to know what they were saying.

A little dust devil suddenly came skipping along by the side of the train, causing the ladies to clutch at their skirts and bonnets. A man lost his hat and went chasing it, but Longarm wasn't watching him. The dust devil had caught Janice's skirt just right and lifted it enough for Longarm to get a glimpse of pink silk stockings and just the least sight of a spangled garter at the middle of her thigh.

He smiled. He wanted a much closer look.

But now, what with all he'd heard, it sounded as if the two wouldn't be spending enough time in Alpine for him to get to know the gal. That in itself was enough to make him want to take a hand and have a look into whatever was troubling the pair, especially Carol Ann Foster.

If she was indeed *that* Carol Ann.

Chapter 4

The train was even smaller than he had imagined, only two coach cars and a caboose behind the coal tender and engine. It appeared that most or all of the people had gotten down from the stuffy cars to stretch their legs and watch the trainmen fill up the boiler from the huge water tank. Looking up at it, Longarm reckoned it was near big enough to swim in.

Standing there, he idly looked the crowd over. Besides himself and the two women he'd become acquainted with, it appeared that there were twelve other passengers, three of them women and one a boy in his teens. Outside of the engineer and fireman, the conductor seemed to constitute the whole train crew. Longarm didn't figure the railroad was exactly getting rich off their Odessa-to-Alpine run, not unless they actually did go on to El Paso with a greatly increased load of passengers.

He looked the group over. With the exception of one or two men in sack suits and foulard ties, who he took to be drummers traveling in farm goods or general merchandise, the rest of the men appeared to be cattlemen of one kind or another. Either the kind that hired or the kind that got hired. A few wore side arms, but most were dressed in the clothes of working men who got their living from the hard land. A few wore narrow-brimmed hats, but the wide brim and the high crown of the cattleman were in the majority.

Janice and Carol Ann were standing off by themselves, a few yards into the desert. Carol Ann had her arms folded, staring at the faraway mountains that seemed to be swathed in blue clouds. Longarm knew they were part of the Davis Mountains, a good three hundred miles away. It was an indication of how clear and thin the air was and how flat the prairie was that the human eye could see so far.

Janice was trying to talk to her, but Carol Ann obviously wasn't listening. Longarm saw the conductor walking away from the watering operation, heading back toward the coaches. The engineer and fireman had shut the water off and were swinging the long spigot back into the place where it was secured against the water tank to keep it from blowing in the wind. Just then Janice broke off her conversation and started toward the cars. Longarm didn't think it was going to be long before the conductor called for the passengers to reboard. He thought maybe he had a chance to have just a word with Carol Ann before she moved. He took the few steps to her side. As he opened his mouth he thought of calling her by her whole name just to see what sort of reaction he'd get. It might, he thought, shock her into revealing what was behind all the mystery about the mail car and why she was acting like she'd just found out she'd been run over by a wagon. But a little warning bell was going off in his head. She'd want to know how he knew her full name, and he couldn't very well say that Janice had told him, because that was too easily checked and he damn sure didn't want her to know how he really knew. So he just said, "Ma'am?"

For a moment she acted as if she hadn't heard him. Then, with a sort of a sigh, she turned half around. She said, "It's lonely out here, isn't it?"

"You could get lost with no trouble. Don't you reckon we better head on back? Train is fixing to crank up."

She turned and stared down the rails south. "I wonder when another train will be coming back this way."

Longarm said, "Well, that's something you'd have to ask the conductor. But I'd reckon it would be that through train that got out ahead of us this morning. And it wouldn't stop. That is if you were thinking of waiting here to flag it down."

She turned and looked him in the face. She had, he thought, wonderfully large eyes. Hazel they appeared to be. But now they were so clouded with worry and misery it was hard to tell. She said, "How did you know that was what I was thinking?"

He shrugged. "Wasn't hard. You asked the conductor if there was a stop where you could get off before Alpine. Since he told you there wasn't one, I figured you was gonna try and make one for yourself."

"I wonder why they call it the through train."

"It's because it has right of way. Ain't but one set of tracks, but there is more than one train that uses them. That T&RG is the big dog so it gets right away. It don't stop. It's what they call an express."

"But there are no stops anyway."

"That ain't the point. If we was out in front of it and it come up behind us, we'd have to get over on a siding like this one here and stay there until it got on by." He looked at her shrewdly. "That's why it has the mail contract and the mail car."

She looked down at her feet. "Yes," she said dully. "Yes, I can see that now."

55

Behind them Longarm heard the conductor call, " 'Board! *All* aboard!"

"We better go."

She looked around. "Are you sure they wouldn't stop?"

"Why don't you think about it. We'll make at least two more water stops before we get to Alpine, and if circumstances are such that you feel you have to get off the train, why, maybe the conductor can wire ahead and have it arranged for whatever train is northbound to stop and pick you up. It might be you will have to tell him it is a life-or-death situation."

She said tersely, "That will not be difficult."

He escorted her back to the train and helped her aboard. Then he waited while the conductor came up and shut the lower half of the door. Longarm said, "How far behind that express train will we be when we get to Alpine?"

The conductor got out his watch and squinted at it. He said, "Well, we're 'bout three quarters of an hour late as it is. And you can bet your bottom dollar we ain't going to make up no time, not on this train. I figure they'll be in and out ahead of us by some four hours. What is all this interest in that damn express? Is it the mail car again?"

Longarm laughed. "I think I've figured out why that young lady is so all-fire concerned about that mail car. I don't know, you understand, but I got the feeling that car is carrying a letter to her sweetheart that she would just as soon have back."

The conductor cocked his head. "You reckon?"

"Only thing I can figure."

The old man shook his head. "Then the young lady don't know peaches 'bout the United States mail service. She couldn't have got that letter back no matter what. Once you put a letter in the hands of a official mail carrier that ain't yore letter no more. Onliest way she could have got that letter back short of its delivery would have been to hold up the mail car. And she don't look much like doing that."

"No," Longarm said. "I wouldn't reckon."

But as he made his way back to his seat a thought nagged at him. He turned it over in his mind a few times and then dismissed it. The idea wasn't workable. But then he did a strange thing. There was a little space between the end of his seat and the wall of the coach. Using his body to shield what he was about, he leaned down and rummaged in his saddle-bags until he had his Colt revolver with the nine-inch barrel. Still hiding his efforts, he worked the revolver in between his seat and coach wall. It was a snug fit, but he managed to shove it down until it was out of sight. It could be found, but only if one was looking for it. He had shoved it down so that the butt was the first part that would come to hand. It would not come out quick, but it could be gotten to.

As he straightened up he saw that Carol Ann was watching him. There was a kind of haunted look about her face. Her eyes seemed to have darkened and recessed. She said, "Did you ask him, Mr. Long?"

"Ask who what?"

"The conductor. I thought you might have been inquiring after what we talked about."

"Well, no," he said awkwardly. "I, uh, didn't think that was my place. I was just asking him how we was doing on the time."

"What did he say?"

"We're running late. Not quite an hour."

She sighed and looked out the window. "I have to get off this train." It didn't seem to Longarm as if she had said it to him. It seemed more like a statement of fact made aloud to herself. He very much wished she would tell him what was troubling her. There were several direct questions he would like to ask her, but he knew it wouldn't do any good. He

57

scooted over to the very aisle side of his seat. She had her head turned toward the window, her back virtually to him. He said, "Ma'am?"

She didn't move.

He said, "Carol Ann?"

She turned and looked at him. "How did you know that was my name?"

Longarm gestured at Janice. "I heard her call you that. I would have never made so bold as to call you by your given name, but I don't know your family name."

She was still looking at him. "Only Janice calls me Carol. Almost no one calls me Carol Ann. Just a very few special people."

Longarm didn't fumble. He said, "I used to know a girl name of Carol Ann. I reckon the Ann just rose unbidden to my tongue. Forgive me if I have made a blunder."

Her eyes went dull again. "It doesn't matter. What do you want?"

He shrugged. "Well, nothing. You seem so upset. I wanted you to know I'd help if you'd tell me how."

"Forget it," she said. "No one can help me. I've got to get off this train, that's all. Where is that damn conductor?"

"He was still forward in the vestibule last I saw of him. He may have gone up to the engine to talk to the engineer."

The woman got up suddenly. "I'm going to see. It was this damn railroad got me in this trouble, so it will be the damn railroad that gets me out!"

She got up suddenly, and was out the coach door before Longarm could react. He looked at Janice. The little blonde just shook her head. She said, "It's best not to worry about her. Sometimes she can be very headstrong."

"Maybe it will work out for the best."

Janice dropped a shoulder. "I don't know. It's Carol's affair. I'm just with her." She half smiled. "By the way, I

58

sometimes do call her Carol Ann. Other people do too. But it's the one whom she is worried about that calls her that as a regular thing. I would guess that is why she responded as she did."

Longarm said, "How is your cider holding out?"

She reached to the seat beside her and held up the jug. It was only a quarter full. She said, "I'm going to save the rest for later. They have a water barrel at the end of the car, but I can't drink it. What do they put in the water out here, lye soap?"

"It's gyppy," Longarm said. "Got gypsum in it, which is close to lye soap. But these folks is grateful for any kind of water. They'll drink anything that ain't solid." He reached beside him and showed her the bottle of whiskey. He said, nodding at her cider jug, "I could put some backbone in that. Make the ride shorter."

"Oh! I couldn't!"

But Longarm noticed that she cut her eyes toward the door that Carol Ann had passed through. He said, "She's busy arguing with that conductor. Wouldn't take me but an instant and nobody the wiser. I noticed Carol ain't had none of the cider."

"Do you think it would be all right?"

Longarm smiled and held out his hand. "I *know* it will be all right. A person ain't supposed to make these long trips without a little help."

She surrendered her cider, smiling shyly. "I feel so wicked."

"Yeah," Longarm said, smiling back at her and studying her bosom. "So do I." He took the cider, uncorked it, and quickly poured a good measure of whiskey into the apple juice. He figured it was enough to loosen up the stays of Miss Janice's corset, though he didn't reckon she needed one. He passed it back to her and said, "Take you a real good hit right quick. Might have to last you a while so make it a good one."

Janice said, "But what if she smells it on my breath? Carol really doesn't hold with spirits. She can be very strict about some things."

"Hell," Longarm said, "I got the place reeking of the smell of whiskey. As close in together as we all are she won't connect it with you. Go on, top it off."

She didn't hesitate long. "Well, if you say so . . ."

Longarm watched as she swallowed twice and then a third and then a fourth time before she brought the jug down. She let out a sigh. "Aaaah, that was wonderful." Then she leaned to her right to see that the door was still closed. She looked at Longarm and smiled conspiratorially. "I feel ever so much better. And you won't tell Carol."

"Me? Mercy, no." He gave her a wink to cement the bond. "Me and you will have our little secret and no one the wiser."

He very much wanted to ask her why she should be so concerned about what Carol Ann thought and why her strictness should affect Janice, but he thought it was still too early in the game. Neither woman had shown the slightest interest in telling him their business, and he thought that if he were to actively pry they'd clam up like a couple of oysters. He calculated that later, after Janice had a little more of the barleycorn in her, she'd be a little looser of tongue.

At that moment Carol Ann came hurrying back. She sat down in her seat with a displeased look on her face. Both Janice and Longarm looked at her. Finally Janice said, "Carol, what did he say?"

"Well, he's just a horrid man. He said he could telegraph and arrange it but he doesn't want to. He said it would somehow be a reflection on him and on the railroad. I assured him that was not the case, that it *would* be a reflection on him and the railroad if they did *not* arrange to get us off this train and headed back north."

Janice said, "He can do it?"

"Yes. There's a last water stop a hundred miles on this side of Alpine. They are somehow able to tap into the telegraph wires that run alongside the track and send messages. But he assured me it would be no end of trouble and he'd have to charge for it. I told him I did not give a damn how much he charged, but that I absolutely had to get off this train before it reached Alpine! I don't know how many times I had to explain it to the man. Either he is hard of hearing or doesn't speak English. I am not sure which."

Janice said, a little anxiously, "But how can it be arranged? There are no towns."

"I am aware of that, Janice. We will reach that water stop at about six o'clock. We will get off there. We will wait. A northbound train is due at near nine o'clock the best the conductor can figure out. Though, God knows, the attention they pay to timetables it could come an hour early or three hours later. It will have instructions to stop for us. We will get on and that will be that."

Janice looked over at Longarm and hesitated for a moment. She said, "But will it, uh, be in time?"

Carol Ann raised her hands and let them fall in her lap. "I don't know. There is another water stop before that one. At about three this afternoon. I asked him to let us down there but he refused. He said it made him nervous enough letting us off for a three-hour wait, much less one twice that long. I don't see what difference it makes. It's our affair."

Longarm said, "Miss, ain't none of my business, but this is not the safest country in the world for a couple of ladies on their own to be standing around unprotected."

She turned her cool gaze on him. "Believe me, Mr. Long, it is the preferable choice. If you have any influence with

61

that conductor I wish you'd prevail on him to put us off sooner. I tell you, it is vital."

Janice said hesitantly, "Carol, we are just going to be at a water stop? Will it be as desolate as that last one?"

"I would think so. Do you see any change for the better as we go south? If anything the country is going from bad to worse."

"But we'll be in the dark. It will get dark very soon after six."

"Are you afraid of the dark, Janice?"

Longarm said, "Ladies, this is rough country. If nothing else, there are enough wild animals hereabouts to fill a zoo. And that's just the four-legged kind. Some pretty rough old boys, Indian and otherwise, hang out in this country."

She put her hand on her purse. "I am armed, Mr. Long."

He looked at the size of her purse. He said doubtfully, "Can't have much of a weapon in there. You got a derringer?"

She said, "I have a Colt, ladies' model, .25-caliber revolver."

".25-caliber, huh?" He got out a cigarillo, lit it, and then reached around and got the bottle of whiskey and had a drink, giving Janice a wink as he did. "Well, that might stop a squirrel or a rabbit, unless they were real determined. Mind telling me what kind of reason you gave the conductor for asking him to make these here kind of arrangements? I don't reckon I ever heard tell of it before and, in case I have need to pull the same stunt, I'd like to know the ways of such a matter."

She looked severe. "I can assure you this is not a stunt. As to what I told the conductor, well, I don't think that matters."

Janice was holding the bottle of cider on her lap. While she listened to Carol, without taking her eyes off her friend's

62

face, she uncorked the bottle of cider and whiskey and took a long pull. Longarm suppressed a smile. To cover any smell of whiskey he hurriedly took another straight pull off his own.

Carol said, "I think we will simply get off at the next stop and refuse to get back on. The conductor can wire or not as he likes. If we have to we'll signal the train."

Janice said worriedly, "But Carol, it will be night."

"Then we'll build a large bonfire. We will think of something. But we have to get off this train as soon as possible. I've made my mind up so there's no use talking about it."

Longarm got out his watch and consulted it. He said, "Well, you've got some time to give it a little thought. My watch says it's lunchtime, but since we ain't got nothing to eat, I reckon we'll just call it twelve noon and let the matter stand at that."

Janice said, a little vaguely, "You'd think they'd arrange to have some sort of food on these trains. On the civilized lines in the East they have actual dining cars. It's like dining in a fine restaurant. What is the matter with these people down here?"

Longarm smiled. "Ain't nothing the matter with them. It's just that they wouldn't know what to do with such frills. Most folks expect the railroad to carry them from place to place. They bring their own grub. You put a restaurant car on one of these Western trains and try and charge two dollars for a meal. Wouldn't get one taker out of every twenty passengers."

Carol was staring straight ahead, not paying any attention except to the thoughts inside her own mind. But Janice said, "Why, that's silly. Doesn't it cost the same to dine in the restaurants hereabouts?"

"They are a little hard to find, restaurants," Longarm said. "There's a cheap cafe here and yon, but mainly a man gets himself a plate of beans or stew or chili in a saloon. Lots of saloons, damn few cafes."

"What are the women expected to do? They can't go into saloons. Not ladies."

"Damn few ladies out here. Them that are here are married and got a kitchen of their own."

Outside the window the country was roughing up. Hard-ridged little hills were appearing, and buttes and knolls, and here and there the land was slashed with ravines and cuts and deep canyons. They were beginning to reach the caprock of the high plains. If the country had been desolate before, it was about to worsen and deteriorate.

Longarm leaned his head back against the seat cushion. There were very few things he could say for sure, but one of them was that he was thoroughly sick of train travel. He took a drink of cider and whiskey, lit another cigarillo, and sat there, his eyes closed, resting. He reckoned to take a nap after he finished his smoke. The plight of the girls was interesting, but his body was starting to warn him it could use a little rest. He thought of Molly for a moment, the visual images causing a small smile to break over his face. He had every intention of stopping to see her on the way back.

A half hour later he was suddenly startled out of his doze by a loud *Pow!* He sat up. Janice or Carol had screamed. Janice said, "It's a gunshot! Someone is shooting at us."

Carol had her mouth pursed shut, but Longarm could see she had gone white in the face.

Then, a few seconds later, they heard another shot. It sounded as if it had gone off right beneath their coach. Longarm felt the train suddenly begin to slow. Janice said, "It's shooting! It's trouble!"

Longarm said, "It's not shooting, but it's trouble. Those are warning torpedoes. Railroad warning torpedoes."

64

Janice looked at him wildly. "What?"

Longarm said, "They put them on the track to warn the engineer if there is trouble on the track ahead. They are like a big firecracker that explodes when the engine's iron wheels roll over them."

"But-but who could have put them there?"

Longarm was looking out the window. "I don't know. Maybe the train that was ahead of us. Maybe there were some weak sections of track and they laid them down behind them to warn the next train coming to slow down. Two means slow down and I think three or four means to stop. I—"

He was interrupted by another explosion. The train began to slow rapidly.

Carol said, her eyes wide, "We're going to stop, aren't we? We are, I just know it. It's him!"

Then there came a fourth explosion under the train and the engineer began to blast his whistle for an emergency stop. Longarm reached out a hand to steady Janice, who was half out of her seat, but then the engineer locked his brakes and the sudden deceleration slung Longarm back against his seat and pitched Janice into Carol Ann's lap.

The train went squealing along for what seemed an eternity, but was actually no more than ten seconds. The squealing intensified as the train slowed. Longarm had a picture of both the engineer and the fireman putting all their weight on the brake.

Then the train stopped. As it did all the forward momentum reversed itself and it suddenly sagged back. The move threw Longarm forward against the seat facing him and threw Janice back into her seat.

It was suddenly very quiet. Down the aisle he could see the other passengers picking themselves up and setting their belongings to rights. There was a low murmur of questions punctuated by a few muttered curses. Longarm looked out the window. He saw men in blue with gold stripes down their pants legs riding horses with a big U.S. brand on their hips. He said, "Well, things can't be very bad. The army is here. I see cavalry."

Carol Ann said, "Oh, my God! We're too late!"

Longarm looked over at her. "What?"

She turned and looked out the window. "Nothing. You'll find out soon enough."

The rear door of the coach suddenly banged open and a figure in blue came striding up the aisle. Behind him were two troopers in cavalry blue marching with their Springfield rifles at port arms. One stopped at the rear, but the other stayed right behind the man advancing toward where Longarm and the two women were sitting.

Longarm looked at him. His uniform was dusty, but his boots were freshly polished and his belt buckle gleamed, as did the two gold bars on his collars. Longarm had no doubt that he was looking at ex-Lieutenant James Meadows, deserted from the Seventh Cavalry Detachment stationed at Fort Davis, Texas. He was heading straight for Carol Ann Foster. He was wearing buckskin gauntlets, the wings of the gloves sticking straight back over his wrists, the fingers soft and pliant. His eyes were fixed straight on Carol Ann Foster. He came straight to her and said, "Where is the goddamn mail car, Carol Ann?"

His voice was even and steady, but she cringed back as if he were thrusting a red-hot poker in her face. She said, "Oh, James, oh, please. It was a mistake. Please don't hurt me."

Without seeming to make an effort out of it he suddenly backhanded the woman across the face. The blow knocked her sideways, sending her all the way across the seat to the

66

coach wall. Longarm started to rise. He said, "Just a damn minute there—"

But he got no further. The trooper behind Meadows suddenly rammed the butt of his rifle in Longarm's chest, knocking him backwards and knocking the breath from his lungs.

With his left hand Meadows reached out and grabbed Carol Ann by the front of her shirtwaist, dragging her toward him. He said, "Sims, disarm that man." He pointed at Longarm with his right hand. Then he raised his voice. "See that everyone in this car is disarmed. On the double."

Meadows pulled Carol Ann close to his face. A little blood was trickling out of the corner of her mouth. He said, "What happened, Carol Ann?"

She was starting to sob. "It was dark. I thought it was the right train. I didn't know until I'd already sent the wire. I'm sorry, I'm sorry. Oh, please, James, don't hurt me."

He suddenly shoved her back into the corner hard. He said, "We're going to look in the caboose, Carol Ann. For your sake I hope the money is there."

Then he straightened up. As he turned his eyes fell on Longarm. He stopped and said tonelessly, "If you try and interfere again, mister, I'll have you taken outside and shot."

Longarm just stared back at him, content for the moment to bide his time and watch for an opening.

Meadows held his gaze on Longarm for a moment longer, looking at him hard as if he sensed some danger. But then he broke off to stare down the coach where his men were busy collecting guns and other weapons from the male passengers. Meadows said, "You men had better not miss anything. If you do you will pay, as well as any passenger who tries to conceal a weapon." He suddenly looked down at Longarm. "You have any other weapons, mister, besides that handgun my trooper took from you?"

Longarm pointed to the overhead rack. "Just that carbine up yonder."

Meadows said, "Sims!"

The trooper was halfway down the aisle, his arms loaded with guns and rifles. He turned, "Yes, sir!"

Meadows reached into the rack over Longarm's head and retrieved Longarm's carbine. He said, "You missed one, Sims."

The trooper looked uncomfortable. He was chewing tobacco and he shifted his cud nervously. "I wuz gonna make 'nother sweep, Lootenant."

Longarm noticed that Meadows was still wearing the regulation U.S. Army holster. It had a flap to keep the revolver from accidentally being dislodged. Meadows had the flap down but it wasn't fastened. Longarm figured the man didn't bother to use his own pistol. He had men with rifles for the work of shooting people.

Meadows said, "Report yourself to the corporal. One demerit."

"Yessir."

Meadows was about to walk away when Janice clutched at his blouse. He stopped and glanced down at her. He said, "Remove you hand, Janice." He said it with no tone in his voice.

She said, "James, you've got to believe Carol Ann. It wasn't anyone's fault. Let her explain. Please."

He fixed her with a look. "I am not interested in explanations, Janice. I am interested in approximately one hundred and fifty thousand dollars in army payroll money. Do you understand?"

She lowered her eyes. "Yes, James."

"Take your hand off me."

She dropped her hand in her lap.

Meadows moved to the center of the car. He faced one

end and then turned and faced the other. He said, "This train is now under my command. Each of you will do exactly as you are told. If there is any hesitation, any interference with me or my troopers, you will be dealt with severely. If you attempt any sort of heroics you will be shot. I have seven highly trained cavalry troopers under my command and they will not hesitate to shoot. Sit still, do not talk, and be patient. Do not leave your seats without permission. If you have needs, such as water or the bathroom, make your needs known to my men. They will be attended to. You have been warned."

Forward, halfway down the coach, a man said, "Hey, feller, just what the hell is a-goin' on here? I mean—"

He got no further. The trooper who had been standing at the rear of the coach rushed forward and clubbed him in the head with his rifle. The man let out a moan and slipped down in his seat until his head had disappeared from Longarm's view.

Meadows turned and looked from eye to eye in the coach. He said, "Next time the trooper will be under orders to shoot. That rifle butt was your last warning." Then he turned on his heel. As he got to the rear door he said, "McKindrick, you will stand post here. Be on your guard or you will pay a reckoning. Sims, you come with me."

Longarm watched him push the door open and disappear, followed by the trooper, his hands and arms full of pistols and rifles and big sheath knives. He thought that if Meadows and his men were deserters, the army was the worse for it. They appeared to be as well disciplined and trained a bunch as he was likely to see in such country. Meadows himself was impressive. Longarm judged him to be nearly a size with himself, though he didn't think Meadows was as heavy. His frame wasn't as big, and Longarm took him at most to be in his early thirties. His age, like the information

69

on Carol Ann Foster, was in Longarm's saddlebags. He could only hope they would not examine them too closely. If they discovered he was deputy United States marshal, he reckoned his life would be forfeit.

James Meadows, he decided, was going to be a handful. The man was very obviously intelligent and very obviously ruthless. But he certainly didn't appear to be a man who could be moved to wrong thinking by anger or emotion. He was quiet, authoritative, and hard. Even the slap he'd given Carol Ann had been passionless. It had been a gesture of punishment, nothing more, nothing less.

But at least the riddle about the mail car was solved. The mail car was supposed to have been, and probably had been, carrying the payrolls for the several army forts in the Southwest area. It would have been the money for Fort Mason, Fort Concho, Fort Stockton, Fort Davis, and probably Fort Bliss in El Paso. Longarm could easily see how it could have amounted to the $150,000 that Meadows had mentioned. And somehow, either Carol Ann or Janice, or both of them, had known about its shipment, most probably out of a bank in Austin since that was the headquarters for the federal district in Texas. They had known which train it was going on and Carol Ann had wired that information to James Meadows at some prearranged hideout. There weren't many towns with a telegraph office within riding distance of the railroad tracks from Odessa to Alpine, but he had somehow been sent word. And he and his men had ridden and stopped the train by putting the torpedoes on the track, and then had discovered it had not been hauling the mail car containing the payroll money. And the payroll would have been all in gold because the inhabitants of the parts of the country that the forts occupied didn't put much stock in paper money.

And Carol Ann had gotten it wrong. Now, having seen James Meadows and his methods, Longarm could easily see why Carol Ann had been so frightened. He was surprised, in fact, that she'd even gotten back on the train after the first water stop. Meadows was now looking for the gold in the caboose. Well, Longarm thought, he was looking in vain. That gold was four hours ahead of them in the strongbox in the mail car aboard the southbound T&RG. All they had here was a dinky train with fifteen poor passengers and not much else in the crew. The whole thing, locomotive and all, wasn't worth a hundred and fifty thousand dollars. Longarm could only hope that Meadows would soon see the futility of his mission and ride on without causing further damage or killing anyone.

He glanced over at Carol Ann. She was sitting straight up in her seat. She'd wiped away the blood from her lip, but he could see where her mouth was swollen. Her eyes were swollen also. He couldn't be sure if that was from crying or from the blow. He said gently, "Carol Ann . . ."

She slowly turned to look at him. He said, "Is that why you wanted off the train so bad?"

She looked at him a long moment. She said, "I . . ." She stopped and closed her mouth and turned her head. She sat there, staring straight toward the end of the car.

Longarm looked at Janice. He said, "I figure that now I've got the right to inquire into this business. These men are as dangerous as any I have ever seen. That man wearing the second lieutenant's bars knows you and he damn sure knows Carol Ann. Something was said about an army payroll. That gets carried in a mail car, I would reckon. It was your business before and I wasn't going to inquire, but now it is the business of every person on this train. Carol Ann is not acting like she wants to talk about it, but I am going to have to have some answers."

Janice looked at him, her face flushed, her lower lip trembling. She seemed on the point of answering, but then she glanced at the set face of Carol Ann and stammered out, "I can't tell you."

"Can't or won't? He damn sure knows the both of you. And I heard you call him by name. James. James what?"

She just shook her head.

Longarm said, "They are dressed as cavalry soldiers, but they are not acting on government business here and now. Where did they get those uniforms? Did they steal them? Are they outlaws?"

Longarm was not about to let on that he knew the whole story. He was going to force it out of the women so he could come by it naturally in their eyes.

Janice just shook her head again. "I can't talk about it."

Longarm gave her a hard look. "I'll tell you something that strikes me funny. These men act like soldiers. That lieutenant, he acts like an officer. And the men take orders from him as if he were an officer. There is something fishy here, mighty fishy. Are these men by any chance deserters? Or maybe they are on a long patrol and just decided to rob a train. Which is it? Dammit, I've got a right to know. That bird at the end of the car looks like he'd just as soon shoot someone as laugh. I'm going to have the answers. You can bet on that."

She didn't answer his question directly. Instead she said hesitantly, "What—what—what makes you think they might really be soldiers? And not just, uh, outlaws who have stolen some uniforms."

Longarm said grimly, "The way that man who's dressed as a lieutenant wears his side-arm, that's what. That's one thing."

She swallowed. "I don't think I understand you."

"He wears it casually. With the flap unbuttoned, but still covering the butt of his revolver. He ain't got it in his hand. He didn't come on this train with it drawn."

72

She said hesitantly, "I still don't understand."

"Don't you?" He gave her a hard look. "Then I'll spell it out for you. He come on this train like he had complete faith in those men behind him carrying the rifles. He come on this train like he didn't have to protect himself, like it would be done for him. Outlaws, robber bands, don't have that kind of discipline. The man is an officer or has recently been one. And the men with him have served with and for him for a long time. You don't get that kind of trust and discipline in outlaw gangs. Now do you understand me? You and Carol Ann there, who has suddenly come down with a bad case of lockjaw, know considerable about this business, and you are going to tell me because my life and the lives of a lot of other people are hanging in the balance here."

He was talking hard, but low, not looking at Janice or Carol Ann, but staring straight ahead so as not to give the guard at the end of the car any call to pay him attention.

He said, "I was willing to be polite and not inquire into your business before, but that was then. That was before that bunch come on board this train. And ain't no use either one of you saying you don't know them because you do. That lieutenant, if he is such, is who Carol Ann was trying to run away from." He turned his head and looked at Carol Ann and then at Janice. "I'll give you a little while to decide. But after that I am going to inform that man you call James that you two were asking to be let off this train after you found there was no mail car. The conductor will back me up. Think about it."

It made Janice draw in her breath with a sharp sound. He saw Carol Ann turn her face toward him. But he just sat back in his seat and had a drink of whiskey.

It was Carol Ann who spoke. "You can't mean that!"

Longarm looked over at her. "Like hell I can't, lady. I don't know what you are playing at here, but I got a good idea you've had a major hand in this. Wittingly or not, willingly or not, I couldn't say. But your past actions belie that you didn't know this was coming. No wonder you wanted off this train and were willing to spend hours alone in this country. I don't blame you. If I'd of knowed the cavalry was on the way, this kind of cavalry, I'd of wanted off this damn train myself, even it I'd had to spend the night in the middle of a wolfpack."

Her eyes were wide and frightened. "But you wouldn't tell James? Surely! It would make him very angry."

"Lady, he don't appear to be exactly happy with you right now."

Her eyes flashed for a second. "Only a cur would stoop so low."

"Listen, Carol Ann, I've watched you for going on better than half a day playing first the Miss High-and-Mighty and then the outraged victim of disaster and finally a treed coon." He stuck out his finger and pointed it at her. "You are going to tell me what this is all about or I am going to tell James, next time I see him, about your plans to leave whatever scheme y'all was in together."

He was going to say more when the trooper on guard, McKindrick, yelled back, "You lot at the back. Shet yore traps. Lootenant said no talkin'. So shet it up!"

Longarm gave her a final look and then settled back in his chair. He said softly out of the corner of his mouth, "Bear in mind what I said. I wouldn't be too long about it."

He heard her make a little sob, but he didn't look her way. The guard couldn't actually hear them. So long as they kept facing forward or didn't look at the other, they could talk freely.

He finished up the last of his cider and whiskey, lit a cigarillo, and thought half humorously about his last conversation with Billy Vail. He had claimed there was more chance of a successful revival being held in a whorehouse than there was of him finding the deserters. He'd said, "Do you have any idea of how big that country is, Billy? You sit here in this office of yours and think it's a long ways down to the cafe. There are huge herds of cattle been lost in that country so long they are still creating sandstorms and they can't be found. What do you reckon, that this James Meadows is just going to come riding up and present himself to me and apologize for causing everybody so much trouble? Why are we wasting manpower on this? Give me something that is possible to do, like making honest men out of every sheriff in every county in Texas."

He smiled to himself. James Meadows had found *him* instead. Of course he hadn't ridden up and surrendered, hadn't even said he was sorry for all the trouble he'd caused, but there was still time.

When his cigarillo was half smoked he said, without turning his face, "Time is passing, lady. How long do you think it is going to take him to search a caboose for a hundred and fifty thousand dollars in gold? When he finishes he is going to come back here. You got that long."

He could see Janice. He saw her bend slightly forward, "For God's sake, Carol Ann, tell him! What difference can it make now?" She stopped and waited. Carol Ann did not say a word. Janice said, "Then the hell with you. I'll tell him!"

"Janice, don't you dare!"

"How could it be any worse? You haven't done anything wrong. I certainly haven't. But if this gentleman tells James what we were going to to . . ." She let the sentence drag to an ominous end. "You know how James can be. He wouldn't even be angry. He's beat you before, Carol Ann. You remember what that was like?"

Carol Ann said, "This man cannot help us."

75

"No, but I can damn well hurt you."

"You wouldn't be so low."

"Lady, you don't understand. I ain't going to take a whipping the same as you when it was you kicked over the milk bucket. I just got on this goddamn train as a passenger. I didn't know I was walking into a robbery of some kind. And you are a part of it. I'll be damned if I'm not going to know what is about to get me killed."

There was a long pause, and then Carol Ann said, "Tell him if you please. I'm having nothing to do with it."

Janice looked at Longarm. She said, "It's a long story. Carol Ann grew up with James in Maryland. I think she's always been in love with him. But all of this really started two years ago when James came to Washington, D.C., to get his commission and his medal for his heroics in an Indian fight. I guess you could say that is what brought us to this day. Carol Ann and I are, uh, in business there. In Washington, D.C."

Chapter 5

Longarm said, "What kind of business?" Though he was already pretty sure he knew.

Janice looked uncomfortable. "Uh, Carol Ann operates a sort of social house, you might say. A . . . a house of recreation that caters to the officers in the capital."

Carol Ann said in a tired voice, "I'm a madam in a whorehouse. We get mostly officers in there on account of the prices we charge."

Longarm looked at Janice. He said, "I reckon I'm looking at one of the reasons only an officer can afford to trade there."

Janice blushed, but Carol Ann said, "Yes. But Janice and I were friends before. She's special. She makes her own decisions, chooses her own gentlemen callers. The others don't have a choice."

Longarm smiled. "So you do business inside of a business."

Janice blushed again. Longarm thought she did an uncommon amount of blushing for a whore, even a selective and high-priced one. She said, "Carol Ann will insist on calling it a whorehouse. I have asked her to refer to it by its French name, a brothel."

Carol Ann said, "What difference does it make? You still do the same thing for the same price."

Longarm said, "Ladies, as fascinated as I am by the nature of your work, I think our time is a little short. I wish you would please get on with the business at hand."

Carol Ann said in a kind of tired voice, a hopeless voice, "James had directed me to have my ladies tell me anything the officers that visited us said. He said that information was power and that power was money. James was sick of the army. He wanted out but he felt like the army owed him more than the paltry salary they had paid him over the years. Shall I go into details about that? It involves the way James hates. James is a very good hater." She said it with a certain grimness that made Longarm think she was talking to herself as much as to him.

He said, "No. I just want the knowledge of how this all worked out. This train business."

Janice answered. "James came home about six months ago on furlough. While he was there I happened to mention that one of my special gentlemen was a major in the Paymaster Corps. He had told me, with some regret, that he would not be visiting me for some time, perhaps as much as two months, because he had to go down to Texas and straighten out the Southwestern Pay District. He said it was a mess, that some of the forts were being paid late and some were missing their pay for extended periods of time and then the right sums weren't being sent. He was going down to consolidate the system and simplify it. When I told James about it he got very excited and ordered me to get all the details I could about the new system and have Carol Ann pass them on."

"So that is what you did?"

She nodded. "Yes. One central system was set up in Austin to pay all the forts south and west of Austin at the same time. Carol Ann wrote James all the details."

Longarm said, still acting as if he only knew what they were telling him, "So then I assume he deserted?"

Carol Ann said, "Yes. All the plans were made by letter and by telegram through a code we had worked out. Because he had been in the ranks he was able to persuade some of the malcontents to come with him. Well, they could hardly be called malcontents anymore than James could."

Longarm said, "But they were looking for an opportunity?"

"Yes."

Janice said, "I would think you know the rest."

"You got on the wrong train."

"Worse than that."

"Carol Ann wired him to stop the wrong train."

"Yes." Janice looked down at her hands.

Longarm said, "What do you think he will do now? James? What is his last name?"

Janice sighed. "I don't guess it matters. Does it, Carol?"

"No. Nothing matters much now."

"Meadows. His last name is Meadows. And he really was a hero. He got a medal and what they call a battlefield commission. He had been a sergeant before that."

"Yes, but the question is what will he do now?"

Janice shook her head. "I don't know."

Longarm said, as if she wasn't present, "What does Carol Ann think?"

Janice sighed again. "She doesn't know either. She has always wondered if James really loved her or if he was just using her." She got a painful look on her face. "Sometimes he . . ." She stopped. "That doesn't have anything to do with this."

"What is it? You have to tell me as much as you can. The more I know the better able I will be to deal with this situation."

Janice looked at him strangely. "You? How do you propose to deal with it? Are you a lawman of some kind?"

Longarm saw his mistake too late and hastened to mend it. "Lawman? Hell, no! But I'm a gambler, a poker player, and you don't ever want anybody better to assess a situation for you than a poker player. I'm a man used to risks, used to calculating the odds. I've stayed alive and I've stayed where I could reach in my pocket and always find money by knowing who and what I was up against."

Carol Ann suddenly said harshly, "Tell him, Janice. Tell him what a fool I've been. Tell him how I gave him money and, and . . ." She stopped.

Janice said lowly, "Sometimes he acted like he preferred the girls who worked for Carol Ann over her. He was always making her send for one for him."

Longarm didn't much doubt it. But he did see how Carol Ann might resent such behavior. He said to Janice, "You?"

She shook her head quickly. "Oh, no! Carol Ann and I have been friends since we were children. Not even James would push matters that far."

"What are his weaknesses?"

Carol Ann said, "He doesn't have any."

"Doesn't have a taste for whiskey?"

"A little, but it doesn't mean much to him."

"Can he be goaded to anger?"

Janice smiled and shook her head. "Not James. He never gets angry. He may want you to think he's angry when it serves his purposes, but only then."

Carol Ann said, "He is completely selfish. He has no feelings. He calculates everything to his advantage."

Longarm said, "How long have you known this?"

80

Her voice was despairing. "From the first. You want to ask me how I could love such a man, do his bidding? I . . . I wish I could answer you." There was a hint of a sob in her voice.

Longarm said gently, "What is he likely to do now?"

Carol Ann said dully, "Oh, I don't think you have anything to fear, Mr. Long. James only kills for profit or punishment. When he is certain there is no gold on this train, he will take what profit he can from the rest of you and kill me for punishment. Then he and his men will ride away. There would be no profit in killing a trainload of people, and it would only make the authorities outraged and more determined to catch him. All you have to do is sit quietly and do as you're told. You'll be safe."

Longarm said, "At some point, when we see a safe chance for you to pass it across, I'll be wanting that little gun you've got in your purse. That little .25-caliber gun."

She shrank back almost physically in her chair. She said, "I'll do no such thing. You're not to have that gun."

Longarm said, "Well, you ain't going to use it. Even when he hit you I saw the way you looked at him. You're scared out of your wits of him, but you'd rather have a blow from him than a caress from another man."

Janice said boldly, "Save your breath, Mr. Long. I've been telling her that for years. So have other people. You can't reach her."

Longarm said, "The man has to be stopped. They've taken all my weapons. You've got to give me that little pistol of yours."

"I am not going to give you the means to murder my fiancé."

"Oh, bull," Longarm said. "He's no more your fiancé than he's mine. Do you want him going on with this?"

"No, but . . . But . . ."

"But what? You tell me the man is mean as a rattlesnake, you tell me he will stop at nothing, but you won't give me any help." She could not know it, but Longarm was not arguing to get the gun in his possession so much as to get it out of hers. He'd as soon throw rocks at the troopers as fire a little popgun like a .25-caliber ladies' model at them. He was afraid, if Meadows took it into his head to whip up on her some more, that she might come out with the little pistol and try and shoot him. He figured all she had to do was bust one cap and there'd be lead flying all over the little coaches.

She said, almost in tears, "Don't ask me to do it. I can't. Not against James. I know what he's doing is wrong and I know some innocent people might get hurt, but I can't help it."

Longarm said, in some disgust, "You remind me of the robber who's lately got a dose of religion standing outside the bank he's fixing to rob saying, 'Lord, deliver me from evil. But not right now.' " He gave her a hard look. "When is gonna be the right time, Carol Ann, to break yourself out of that man's clutches? He's taken your affections, your money, and he's liable to take your life."

He heard her draw her breath in sharply. Her eyes were no longer on his face, but were staring at the end of the car. James Meadows had come through the back door and was striding straight for them. He looked neither to the left nor the right, but came straight to the seats where Carol Ann and Janice sat. He moved close to Carol Ann, staring down at her. Longarm studied him, thinking what an ideal soldier he looked and how pleased his superiors must have been with him, and then how startled they would have been when it became clear he had deserted. He reckoned they'd been a long time in coming to believe it.

Meadows said, staring down at the shrinking young woman, "There is no gold on this train, Carol Ann. The conductor

82

has convinced me that, since the Texas and Rio Grande has the mail contract, the money would be on that train. A fact that should be plain to a child." He suddenly backhanded her with his right hand, knocking her head and shoulders halfway out into the aisle. But then he slapped her back to his left with an open-palmed slap with his heavy gloved hand. The blow knocked her back into the corner. Blood was running from her mouth and nose. He said, "I will have my money, Carol Ann. You are an ignorant, careless whore, but I will have my money."

Longarm said quietly, hoping to distract the man before he could hit the young woman again, "Well, at least you've got your courage."

Meadows whirled on him. His hard gray eyes were fixed on Longarm the same way he'd looked at the woman. "What? Did you say something to me?"

Longarm said easily, "Yeah, I said I see you still had your courage. Ain't everyman can get up the nerve to knock a one-hundred-twenty-pound woman around."

Meadows stared at him for a long second. "Who are you?"

"Name is Long, Custis Long."

"And what is your business, Mr. Long?"

"I'm a gambler by trade. Poker mostly."

Meadows said grimly, "Right now, Mr. Long, you are gambling with your life when you stick your nose into matters that are none of your affair. I do not make a practice of hitting women. But this woman has sorely let me down. She has failed me, and in failing me, she has failed the men I lead. That could undermine my authority."

Longarm thought, so he does have a weakness. Pride. He is eaten alive with it. Why else would a man desert the cavalry and then continue to look and act like he was a serving officer. And why would he be so concerned about his authority over a bunch of outlaws? These men were no longer deserters; they were bank robbers and train robbers. But he said, "Wasn't being critical. Been a lot of women I'd of like to have give a lick or two. Just never had the nerve. Public opinion, don't you know. Takes a courageous man to fly in the face of public opinion."

Meadows stared at him as if trying to decide if Longarm was making sport of him or not. Finally he contented himself with saying softly, "I'll be keeping an eye on you, Mr. Long. Depend on it."

Then he turned and addressed himself to the coach. "I want your attention!" He waited until those who had been dozing or who were slumped down in their seats had straightened up and were being attentive. He said, "This train is about to move backwards. We are going to back up for about five miles. Some work will be done and then we'll move forward again. I know you are getting impatient and uncomfortable staying in your seats. And this car is getting overly warm. As soon as we have completed a necessary task, we will bring the car forward to where it will stay for the time being. Once there you will be allowed to get off and stretch your legs."

Then, without another word, he turned and left the car at the forward end toward the engine and coal tender.

Janice said, looking mystified, "What in the world is he about?"

Just then the train started with a jolt and began backing slowly down the track. Longarm said, "He's going back five miles to tear up the tracks. I imagine he's already done that ahead. That was the reason for the warning torpedoes."

"But why would he do that?"

Longarm said, "I'm not a military man, but I can guess at his reasoning. He can't keep the fact of this train being stopped secret, forever. Sooner or later somebody is going

84

to come to investigate. And when they do he doesn't want them to be able to get close. Let's say he's got the track torn up ahead for three or four miles and he's going back five to tear up the track there. If he gets right in the middle he can't be surprised, not on this flat terrain. I don't know what he's up to, but he don't act like he's leaving." He turned his head in spite of the guard at the other end of the car. "Carol Ann, what do you make of it? What do you think he's got in mind?"

She just shook her head quickly and dabbed at the blood still leaking out of her nose. Longarm could see where the flesh around her eyes and nose was starting to swell. Little runlets of tears were making furrows through the powder and rouge she was wearing on her cheeks. She started to speak, and then shook her head again and looked out the window.

Longarm said, "He says he will have his money. If there ain't none I don't know where he's going to get it. Maybe he's going to wire the railroad and ransom their train back to them." He said it jokingly, but he wasn't so sure, on reflection, that he wasn't right.

Janice said, "I'm scared, Mr. Long."

He nodded. "So am I. Carol Ann, your fiancé scares the hell out of me. Has he always had the funny glint in his eye?"

She said, turning to look at him, "I don't know what you mean." But the words did not come out precisely through her bruised lips.

He said, "When he was staring at me I noticed something that just didn't look quite right in his eyes. Wasn't anything you'd normally notice, but there is a look in them that is just a little off. I've seen that same look in men who are born killers. They are missing a part of some kind. You cannot expect them to act like you or me or a normal person."

85

She said fiercely, "James is not crazy, if that is what you are implying."

Janice said, "For God's sake, Carol, are you going on defending the man? What else does he have to do to you before you come to your senses?"

For answer she put her wadded handkerchief to her mouth and cried into it.

Longarm looked at them now with new eyes. He understood why he couldn't place them as either quality or trash; mainly because they were both. Not that he had anything against a good, honest whore; it was more that they had been masquerading as honest, genteel women and it hadn't quite come off.

The train stopped. In the quiet Longarm could hear the low chuffing of the engine. He heard noises from the rear of the train and shouts and, now and again, the sound of steel against steel. He reckoned they were dismantling several sections of track and bending them with horsepower.

Soon enough the commotion ended and the train started forward again. Longarm said to Carol Ann, "I am going to have to have that pistol of yours. If you don't give it to me I'll tell James Meadows you have it."

With a sudden move Janice reached across the space between them and grabbed Carol Ann's purse. She hid it under her skirt. She said to Longarm, "I'll get it to you when it's safe."

Carol Ann said, her voice choked with tears, "You have no right."

"Carol, it's all over. James is not your lover anymore, if he ever was. He is an enemy. And I'm beginning to think like Mr. Long. I think he might be crazy. I can see him robbing this train if there were gold on it and then riding off. But there's no gold and he is making plans to do God knows what. I'm scared and I think Mr. Long is our best chance. I don't know if you've noticed, but he's the most capable-looking man on the train."

She looked at Longarm as she said the last and he gave her a small wink. "Don't worry," he said. "We'll figure something out."

Carol Ann said coldly, "All right, Mr. Long, now that you may have armed yourself at my expense, exactly what do you intend to do? Are you going to shoot James?"

Longarm scratched his jaw where a day's growth of whiskers had sprouted. "No, I ain't going to shoot James Meadows. Not unless I want to get filled full of lead by them folks he's got with him. As to what I'm going to do, I can't say. This situation is like a poker game. Right now your fiancé is holding most of the chips. I got damn few and ain't drawn a winning hand in some time. So I'm going to do what any smart poker player would do. I'm going to bide my time until I see a little luck starting to run my way. When that will be, I don't know." He gave Carol Ann a glance. "I do know I ain't going to take possession of that pistol of yours until I'm sure you won't make one last try at winning your sweetheart back by telling him I've got it hid under my hat."

Janice said, "Carol Ann! You wouldn't do something like that? Would you? Can't you finally get over him? Can't you see he is slowly beating you to death? What will it take, his fist? I have been your friend for a long, long time and I've seen how much you've thrown away for that man. When are you going to see he's not the boy you fell in love with? I think Mr. Long is right. I think something is wrong with him. Look at him! He's changed."

For answer Carol Ann just pinched up her face and let two, fat tears roll down her cheeks. She said, "Oh, don't bother me about it. I don't care if he kills me or not. Just leave me alone. Do what you will."

Longarm looked at Janice. She just smiled and shrugged. He said, "That house Carol Ann has in Washington . . . I take it it is pretty high-class?"

"Oh, yes," Janice said. "Only the highest-ranking officers. James could have never got in as a mere lieutenant. We also had congressmen and now and again a senator. Very discreet."

"Then Carol Ann should be rich."

Janice shook her head. "No. It was not a house where the madam did awfully well. She only got a small percentage from the girls. She fronted the place because she looked so . . . so respectable. I'm sure you can see that."

"I see," Longarm said. He laid his head back against the headrest and stared at the ceiling. He had a lot of thinking to do, but not much information to do it with. For the time being he was simply going to have to be patient and look for an opportunity. For all practical purposes the odds were eight to one against him. He didn't expect he could get much help from the other passengers, and wasn't, so far as that went, going to try and solicit any.

The train came to a slow stop. Longarm guessed they were halfway between the two breaks in the track. It seemed that no sooner had the train come to a rest than troopers were running through the cars ordering everyone out on the west or telegraph-line side. Longarm got up with the rest. He noticed that Janice handed her handbag to Carol Ann to carry and tucked Carol Ann's under her own arm, at the same time shooting Longarm a meaningful glance.

Longarm reckoned he'd never seen anything like it. Meadows had all the passengers lined up by the side of the train. Two of the three crew members, the fireman and the engineer, were lined up with them. The steam in the engine had been vented and it sat there, an iron monster, capable of going nowhere even if it could have run across the prairie without benefit of tracks.

Next to the telegraph line the conductor was sitting at a little folding table with a telegrapher's box on it. One of the troopers had shinnied up a telegraph pole and spliced into the line with a bare copper wire. The other end of the wire had been attached to the telegraph key that sat in front of the conductor. Longarm noted that the old man did not look happy. He was sitting on a little folding stool, apparently awaiting instructions.

The troopers, rifles in hand, were ranged along in front of the passengers and the other two crew members. There were seven troopers. Longarm took note of that and wondered where the seventh man, the corporal, had been when they had robbed the bank in San Angelo. He reckoned to ask Meadows, and he had no doubt that Meadows, in the arrogance of being in full control, would tell him the truth. He stood with Carol Ann and Janice near the middle of the line of passengers, wondering what Meadows was up to.

He was not to be held long in suspense. Meadows came out of the caboose, walked over and spoke a few words to the conductor, and then took a few strides and positioned himself in front of the passengers. He said, "Let me have your attention, please. I originally stopped this train with the understanding that it was pulling a mail car that contained the payroll for a number of forts in the general area of southwest Texas. It has turned out that that car is on another train. I had expected to profit by the amount of that payroll, which I have reason to expect was about one hundred and fifty thousand dollars."

He paused, and there was a stir among the passengers as they took in his information. He let them have a moment and then he said, "Quiet!"

The crowd stilled.

He said, "Being done out of that money I am forced to make other plans, because I will not be robbed of that hundred and fifty thousand dollars. Accordingly, I am going to contact the company that owns this railroad train and ransom it to them." He paused. "You are part of that train. In fact, you are the main part of that train." He paused to let the passengers digest this new information. They seemed stunned. About all they did was look at each other. But the announcement made the hair prickle on the back of Longarm's neck. The thought had passed through his mind that Meadows might try something of this nature, but he'd assumed the man wasn't that crazy.

Meadows said, "Now. The conductor is going to wire his company the news. I have a man among my troops who is an expert telegrapher, but I am told that each telegraph sender has a touch that is like his signature. In other words the people at the other end of this message will know it is the conductor who is sending the message so they will take it seriously. It is my opinion that that is an important point, especially in view of the terms he will be sending. By the way, for those of you who do not know, the conductor's name is J. D. Hatch and he has been on one line or the other for twenty-five years. He was planning on retiring this year."

Longarm muttered out of the side of his mouth to Janice, "This sonofabitch is fixing to get up to no good."

Janice said, "Since you mentioned it I see, more and more, that sort of funny look in his eye."

Longarm said, "I think the sonofabitch is crazy."

Meadows said, "I am telling you all this because you are all directly affected." He paused. When he went on there was no more feeling in his voice than if he'd been talking about the weather. "Mr. Hatch is going to telegraph his company that I demand one hundred and fifty thousand dollars be delivered to me on this spot. In gold."

The crowd made a little murmur.

He said, "My telegrapher will be listening to make sure Mr. Hatch wires my exact words. In addition I am going to have one of you, the passengers, present so that you can all be assured that this matter is being handled straightforward and on the up and up. All I want is what is mine, and no one need fear so long as I get it." He paused and let his eyes run up and down the line. "Now, one problem we face is a shortage of provisions and water. My troops and I have sufficient for ourselves, but we cannot share them with you for the obvious reason that, once we have the money, we will be forced to flee into the desert to escape apprehension, and will therefore need every scrap of food and drop of water. So, for your comfort, I am going to try to force this railroad company to conclude negotiations with me as quickly as possible so that you will not suffer from deprivation of supplies or needed water." He stopped and pulled out his watch. "It is five-thirty P.M. In a moment I will ask Mr. Hatch to communicate my demands. In those demands I am going to make it clear to the company that owns this railroad that I require that money within twenty-four hours or I will be forced to shoot one of you."

There was a stunned silence. Then one man, a heavyset fellow who looked like a banker, suddenly stepped forward. Longarm could see an elk's tooth hanging off the end of his watch chain. He said, "Just who the hell you think you are? You men in the United States cavalry or not? What in hell is going on around here?"

Meadows nodded to a trooper, who walked up to the man and slammed him in the side of the head with the butt of his rifle. The big man went down in a heap, his hat flying off the side of his head. He lay where he'd fallen, not moving.

Meadows looked at the stunned crowd. "Now, will there be any more interruptions? I don't like to be interrupted when I am speaking. When I am through you may feel free to ask any questions, though I doubt you will have any. I make myself clear as a general rule. Now, as I was saying, I am going to give the railroad company twenty-four hours— we'll call it until six P.M. tomorrow evening—to deliver me the money. If it has not arrived by then I will shoot a passenger. I will then give them another twenty-four hours, and if the money has not arrived, I will shoot another passenger." He looked slowly down the line. "Is that understood? It is not complicated, so I can't see where you should have any questions. You are my hostages. I intend to use you to get money out of the railroad. What could be simpler than that?"

He looked down the line, as if expecting someone to argue with his logic. He said, "So. We are agreed. One thing I want to warn you against, and that is any attempt to attack me or my troopers. If you do that we will kill you, but we will do it in a cruel way. Even though you outnumber us you are not organized and we are. You are not soldiers and we are. You are not armed and we are. You would not have a chance. Are there any questions yet?"

He waited, but no one said anything. They looked too shocked. The man who had been bludgeoned by the rifle butt was still lying on the ground.

Meadows said, "For your information, we deserted a little over two weeks ago and have been hunted hard since. Since the United States is technically at war with the Apache nation, our desertion is punishable by hanging. You can see from that that we have nothing to lose. But you do." He let that sink in before moving on. He said, "There are fifteen of you passengers. I estimate I will only have to shoot three of you before the railroad capitulates and sends me my money.

They face total ruin if they don't. Now three out of fifteen gives you pretty good odds. We have a gambler here, a Mr. Long, who can tell you that. I mention this because some of you may be contemplating escape. Let me say that you are free to go. Wander off right now, right into the middle of this desert. You are at least fifty miles from the nearest water and God only knows how far from the nearest food and shelter. If you want to escape we will not stop you, but you will have reduced your odds to zero." He looked straight at Longarm. "Do you agree, Mr. Long?"

Longarm stared back at him for a moment, unwilling to participate in any statements this madman made. But he finally said, "I'd say that was about the size of it."

Meadows said, "So you see? Now, as to rescue. We have torn up the tracks so that no train can get within five miles of us. That means that any rescue force would have to come overland for at least five miles. In that distance, over this flat terrain, we could cut them to pieces, even if they were a force of two hundred. I've got seven expert marksmen that can hit a target at a thousand yards with the Springfield rifles they carry. The losses we could inflict on any rescue party would be unacceptable, and that's just to get to us. Once here they would have no cover, and we would be barricaded in the train and the locomotive. So you see, do not look for help from any direction except the railroad's cooperation in bringing me my money. Once I have that, we will leave you in peace and go our way. You will have been inconvenienced, but you will still be alive." He stopped and looked at Longarm. "Mr. Long, would you please join me for our first message that Mr. Hatch is going to transmit to his company headquarters. As an obviously well-traveled man of the world, I think you will be an ideal witness that I am simply putting forward a straight business deal. Come forward now."

Longarm glanced at Janice and shook his head slightly. This sonofabitch, he thought, is crazier than I reckoned. He not only plans robbery and perhaps murder, he wants someone to be able to testify he did it in the name of good business.

But nevertheless Longarm walked forward, going to join Meadows and the conductor and Meadows's telegrapher at the little folding table. As he walked forward he surveyed how Meadows had his troopers deployed. They were scattered at strategic points where they could cover all possibilities. He thought to himself that his hidden six-gun wasn't going to do him much good against such an organized force. In the first place he had to somehow get it outside without being detected, and it was too big to secrete about his person. He could probably hide Carol Ann's little popgun under his hat, but that would be like sticking a pin in an angry bull. Every way he looked, it seemed as if Meadows had him cut off from any form of action.

He came up to the group around the little table. He said, "Yessir?"

Meadows said, "You don't by chance, know Morse code, do you, Mr. Long?"

Longarm smiled and shook his head. " 'Fraid not."

"That's all right. You'll hear what I tell Mr. Hatch to send, and my telegrapher is here to make sure he sends my words and my words only. I simply want your presence as a witness to my good intentions. Are you ready, Mr. Hatch?"

The old man looked beaten down. He said, "I reckon so, though I want it noted that I am doing this with a gun at my head."

Meadows said to the trooper that was standing by, "Are you ready, Hanks?"

"Yessir."

Meadows cleared his throat and then said, in a loud voice, "Address this to the president of your company. Tell him I am in control of this train. What train is it, by the way?"

"Old Number 912."

"Very well. Add that I am in control of train Number 912 carrying fifteen passengers and three crew members. Advise him that I cannot be approached by rail or by any other means except with a great loss of life. Advise him I demand he deliver to me within twenty-four hours one hundred and fifty thousand dollars in gold. The gold is to be delivered by one man in a buggy. No other means of transport will be satisfactory. Assure him that once I have this gold in my possession I will go my way. Now send that part."

They all waited while the conductor tapped out the message on his telegraph key. Meadows watched his trooper. Hanks nodded as the conductor sent the message. When the conductor was through Hanks said, "It wasn't the exact words but it was mighty close."

Meadows said, "Now send this." He paused, thinking. "If I do not receive the gold by tomorrow at six P.M., I will kill a passenger. I will kill another one every twenty-four hours thereafter until I either receive the gold or all the passengers are dead. I have with me seven well-armed and deadly subordinates. Your conductor is sending this and I now allow him the freedom to verify what I have said. I expect your answer in one hour."

Longarm stood in awe of the man's arrogance. He not only didn't care for the suffering caused the passengers, he was perfectly certain that the railroad would be compelled to comply with his wishes.

The conductor tapped on for a few minutes and then stopped. He looked up at Meadows. He said, "I reckon you know this is being picked up by every telegrapher that is on this line."

"Doesn't matter," Meadows said carelessly. "What are they going to do? As you can see, my position is very near invulnerable." He waved toward two wagons a little way up the line. Longarm had not noticed them before because the wagons were tethered in a clump of mesquite along with the troopers' horses. Meadows said, "I've got plenty of provisions and water in those wagons. I've got plenty of ammunition and I've got a Gatling gun. Anybody that would be fool enough to advance on me on this flat plain would deserve what they got."

The key in the little box suddenly started chattering. Hanks listened intently and then said to Meadows, "They are checking up to make sure this ain't bogus. They want Mr. Hatch to send some details about his family to authenticate hisself."

"Send it," Meadows said. "I expected them to have suspicions. But Mr. Hatch, I'd be sure they understand how serious this matter is and what an impatient man I am. You should also notify them that the rails are torn up on both sides of us and that the passengers have no provisions and are low on water. Send it."

Hatch bent over his key. When he was through there was a wait of about ten minutes. The key started chattering again. Once again Hanks listened intently. When the key went quiet he said to Meadows, "They say they've got to give the matter some study. They want Hatch to stand by while they get hold of all the officers of the company. They make the point that a hunnert and fifty thousand dollars is a hell of a lot of money."

Meadows laughed. "Well, at least we know we have their attention. Trooper Hanks, stay with the conductor. Mr. Hatch, I'm sorry, but I'm afraid I will require you to stand by your machine until relieved."

Longarm said, "It ain't none of my business, Mr. Meadows, but do you really reckon some dinky little railroad is

96

going to give you that kind of money? Hell, I doubt they got it, and if they do, it will break them."

Meadows turned around so that he was facing Longarm straight on. "You are wrong, Mr. Long. This is very much your business. You may well be one of the ones I shoot. You may well be the first man I shoot. That aside, it is not my concern where they get the money. I rather think that their colleague companies in the railroad business will feel compelled to come to their aid. What is bad publicity for one railroad line is bad publicity for all of them. Now." He raised his voice to address the rest of the passengers and crew. "You are all to return to the coaches while my men and I tend to our animals and draw our provisions." He touched the brim of his hat. "By the way. You would all be advised to address me as Lieutenant. I still wear the uniform and the insignia of my military calling."

Longarm snapped him off a mock salute. "My apologies, Lieutenant." Longarm turned and went back with the people into the coaches. The man who had been hit with the butt of the rifle was in bad shape. He had to be helped by three other men, and even then he stumbled and staggered about. Once he was inside, a few ladies did what they could, washing the wound and binding it with a bandage from a ripped-up petticoat, but it was clear to Longarm that the man was hurt bad. He'd heard a doctor refer to such a condition as a concussion. The doctor had said it was sometimes fatal.

There was a water barrel at each end of the coach. Both, fortunately, were still pretty full, but Longarm took the precaution of filling his cider jug and Janice's jug with the brackish water before somebody decided to use some of it to shave with or take a bath. He didn't know how long they were going to have to wait and the water could be critical.

It grew dark. Through the window Longarm could see the figure of the conductor hunched over his instrument. Occasionally it would chatter, and then Longarm could hear the sound of his reply.

The wounded man was in their coach, and even though he was far in front, Longarm could plainly hear the sounds of his moans and groans.

Janice smiled at him from her seat in the half gloom. "I'm hungry," she said.

Longarm grimaced. "I reckon we'll have to make do with air. I shore wish I'd bought about a dozen more of those ham sandwiches. One would go mighty good right now."

Carol Ann seemed to have slipped into some kind of trance. She sat in the far corner of her seat, her arms crossed, her eyes open, but not seeing anything.

Janice said, hesitating a little, "Do you think I could come and sit by you for a moment?"

Longarm made a motion. "Come on. And welcome. Lord, I never thought you'd ask."

He moved his knees aside so she could squeeze past him and take the window seat. When she was settled she showed him Carol Ann's handbag. "I have her gun," she said.

Longarm sighed. "Well, just hang on to it for the time being. It ain't really going to do much good against that bunch of trained soldiers. Even if I still had the revolver they took off me it wouldn't do much good. There are too many of them for one man and they never bunch up."

"But if you could kill James . . ."

He looked around at her. "That's guessing and that is dangerous. You don't know for sure that the others would quit or leave. One of them is a corporal. He's used to giving orders also."

98

She sat very close to him, taking his arm in both her hands. She said softly, "I feel safer with you."

He smiled. "I feel safer with you too. But mainly I just feel better." He put his hand on her knee as a sort of experiment. When she didn't object, he let it slowly slide up her thigh, letting his fingers curve around until the tips were gently caressing the soft inner flesh. The only move she made was to move closer to him.

He said, "What is Carol Ann gonna think?"

Janice made a face. "She is out of reach right now. Everyone warned her about James, but she was stuck. I only came with her because she begged me and because I hoped I could protect her a little. But you see how it is."

"Yes," he said. "I understand. She ain't takin' it too well."

Janice pushed herself even closer to him. The sun had been down an hour and it was starting to get chilly. "How long do you think this will last?" she said.

He shook his head. "Darlin', I ain't got the slightest idea. The only man as knows that is the one with all the guns."

"Have you thought of anything to do? Any way to stop him?"

He shook his head slowly, sadly. "Janice, I haven't got a single idea that would last more than a minute." He put his left arm around her and pulled her into his chest. His right hand went on exploring up her thigh. "All I know to do is take what comfort we can from each other and try and not worry."

"How do you not worry in a situation like this?"

He smiled quietly at her. "If we had room enough and privacy enough I'd show you."

She put her hand on the fly of his pants. "Guess we'll just have to do the best we can under the circumstances." She turned her face up to be kissed and he brought his mouth down to hers.

"Carol Ann can see us," he said.

Janice said, "The hell with Carol Ann. She's turned to vinegar inside. Let her curdle. God, what a fool she's been. It isn't enough she's let that man ruin her life; now she's drug in better than a dozen innocent bystanders."

Longarm said, "Just scoot down in the seat a little. Maybe we can do more than appears possible."

Chapter 6

At sometime around two o'clock in the morning Longarm was roused from sleep by one of the troopers who shook him roughly awake. In the dim light of the coach he could see it was the corporal with the two gold chevrons on his sleeve. The corporal said, "Git up, mister! Git up right now! The lootenant wants you an' he don't want to wait!"

As gently as he could Longarm disengaged himself from Janice, who seemed curled all over his arms and legs. When he was free from her he stood up slowly, trying to shake the sleep from his brain. As he moved out into the aisle he had one fleeting fear that Janice might find the revolver he had shoved down between the seat cushion and the wall. But he put the thought away. The odds were that she wouldn't find it, and if she did, that she would leave it alone and say nothing about it.

As he got out into the aisle he looked over into the opposite seat. Carol Ann was curled up in a ball, sleeping on the hard seat, her arms and hands clutched up to her neck and her face as if to ward off a dream or a blow or the foul wind of fortune.

He followed the corporal off the train, stepping carefully

down the steps in his half-awake state. It was a good moonlit night, one, Longarm reckoned, in which you could do just about anything you wanted except read a newspaper or a woman's eyes.

Trooper Hanks, Meadows, and the conductor were at the little table. The conductor was slumped over with tiredness. Meadows was striding back and forth briskly. He stopped as the corporal brought Longarm up. Meadows said, "I am sorry to have awakened you, but I want you as witness to the frivolity with which they have received my ultimatum." He gestured at the conductor. "Tell him, Mr. Hatch, tell him! Tell him how they are treating me like a fool!"

The conductor turned weary eyes up to Longarm. He said, "They are asking for seventy-two hours. They claim it will take them that long to get that much gold together and get it here."

Meadows broke in. "Can you imagine that? They must take me for the biggest fool west of the Mississippi! Seventy-two hours, my ass. It won't take them seventy-two hours to get the gold together, but it will take them seventy-two hours to assemble a force strong enough to overrun my position."

Hatch said tiredly, "They have asked him to spare all passengers until that time."

Meadows said, "Of course they have! If I were in their shoes I would have done likewise. Who, I ask you, sir, do they think they are trying to gull? Do I look like a man that easy to deceive? Speak frankly."

Longarm shook his head slowly. "I'd say not. But what if they are speaking the truth? Ain't a hell of a lot of gold in this part of the country. They are going to send to Dallas or Oklahoma City or some big place. A hundred fifty thousand dollars is a power of money."

"It is available," Meadows said grimly. "It is available

and I will not be tricked. Mr. Hatch, if you please, wire them back that their terms are not acceptable. Make note that a representative of the passengers agrees with me, a Mr. Custis Long."

Longarm said, "Now, wait a minute. I ain't said no such thing."

But Meadows waved his protest aside as the key began to chatter under the conductor's practiced finger.

While he was sending the message Longarm said, "You better let Mr. Hatch get some sleep. He ain't as young as he was. You could lose him, and then they might not believe you as readily as they will with messages coming in over his signature."

"You are right," Meadows said. "Mister Hatch, when you finish that message add that this station is closing down and will not reopen until late tomorrow morning."

Hatch paused and then added a phrase or two and let his key fall silent. He closed the wooden lid over the key. He looked up at Meadows. He said, "Sir, again, I hope you are aware that these messages are going out over an open line. Anyone within the reach of these wires could be picking up these messages."

"Of course I am aware of that," Meadows said. "In fact I am pleased by it. It will give the railroad very little excuse if they do not pay us and find all these passengers killed. I don't think it will be very good for their business."

Longarm said softly, "Or yours."

Meadows wheeled on him. "Did you offer a comment?"

Longarm looked him in the eye. "I said I didn't reckon it would be very good for your business to leave a trainload of massacred passengers. It might tend to call close attention to yourself from every lawman from here to the Rio Grande."

Meadows looked at him curiously. "I have practically the

whole of the cavalry stationed in this area hot in pursuit of me and my troop. Do you think I fear a few sheriffs and marshals?"

Longarm shrugged. "Wasn't trying to tell you your business. Was just pointing out something you already taken into account. My mistake."

Meadows said briskly, "I like a man who can admit when he's wrong. You do not run into many of them in the service of the United States Army."

Longarm smiled slightly, but didn't say anything.

Meadows said, "Right. Mr. Hatch, you will take yourself to your quarters. Corporal Cupper, you and Trooper Hanks are relieved. Corporal, wake up Trooper Sims and have him stand guard over this telegraphic equipment the balance of the night. Advise him that this is his punishment for inattention to duty."

"Yessir!" the corporal said. He saluted, and then he and Hanks and the conductor started off.

Longarm said, "Lieutenant, do you mind if I ask you a few questions?"

"Not at all. I have nothing to hide. And I always enjoy the conversation of an intelligent man, which I have discerned you to be."

Longarm let the compliment pass, though he didn't know what he had done or said to give Meadows that impression. "Without prying I came to know a little something about you. I have sat next to those two ladies since Lubbock and—"

Meadows said evenly, "I think you are a little free with the use of the word ladies. But let it go. You don't know their background and, on the surface, I'm sure you've given them the benefit of the doubt."

Longarm said, "Well, whatever. But in the course of our conversation I gathered that one of them was on the way to meet a cavalry officer. I figure that to be you. Am I correct?"

Meadows inclined his head in a nod. "So?"

"Well, the way they talked about you, how you'd been decorated for bravery and received a battlefield commission. It just don't square with all this." He waved his arm to include the train and its passengers. "What I'm wondering . . . With such a future as you have in the cavalry, why would you throw it all away to take up robbery and extortion?"

Meadows fixed him with his hard, pale eyes. "Mr. Long, have you spent the majority of your life taking senseless orders from men who are not fit to black your boots? Have you been forced to carry out strategies that not only were doomed to failure from the time pen was set to paper, but would insure the deaths of many a man who need not have died? Have you suffered the strutting and posturing of some lackey whose commission was bought for him? And were you forced to take orders from that pompous fool only because his family had money? Have you had to follow orders you knew were wrong and smile and say 'Yes, sir!' at the same time? Have you had to smother you own intelligence because it would not be good politics to show up your commander for the fool and idiot he is? Have you ever experienced any of these situations?"

Longarm thought a moment. Finally he shrugged his shoulders. "Well, no, I can't say that I have."

"Then I recommend, until you have, that you hold the question you just asked me. You may find that you already know the answer."

"I can see that part, Lieutenant, but I want to know how you justify killing these people. You paid me the compliment of being intelligent. You don't strike me as lacking in that department."

Meadows smiled a thin-lipped grin. "Mr. Long, you call yourself a gambling man. I will wager you a hundred dollars spot cash that I do not have to shoot more than one of these passengers before the railroad capitulates."

Longarm said, "Lieutenant, I have been known to bet on which fly out of a half a dozen would land first. But I don't reckon I'd care to wager on how many people will need to get killed before the railroad brings you your money."

Meadows looked at him with a thin veil of contempt. "I may have misjudged you, Mr. Long. When you came to the rescue of that whore yesterday I thought it was out of a sense of chivalry. I see now it was just softness."

Longarm smiled crookedly. "You might be right about that. I will admit to having a soft spot in my heart for the ladies. Always has been a weakness of mine."

"Mr. Long, you are dismissed. Or to put it in civilian terms, your presence is no longer required. I'm going to get some sleep. You may stay out or go back as you choose. However, be aware that this perimeter is guarded." He nodded toward the train. On top of the coaches Longarm could see two sentries standing alertly, rifles in hand.

"And Trooper Sims will be along shortly for his punishment tour."

Longarm said, "I can use a little sleep myself."

"Then I bid you good night."

Longarm watched him stride away in his best parade gait. This man, he thought, was a formidable enemy. He was trained, he was desperate, he had good instincts, and he was insane. Watching him duck into the caboose, Longarm decided that Meadows was a man who was going to be hard to catch off guard, and would be extremely dangerous even then.

But something had to be done and done quickly.

Back inside the coach he saw that Carol Ann was still

106

curled up on the seat like a scared little girl. Which, he reckoned, she was. And, he thought, with good reason. He did not expect that Meadows was through with her. If he got his gold after all, he might let her live, but if he didn't, if he had to run or fight, he reckoned things would go hard for Carol Ann. For that reason as much as any of the others, Longarm had to find a way to stop the man. But he just didn't have the weapons for it, not the way the troopers were spread out and positioned. He sat down. Janice was curled up in the far corner. She stirred slightly as he pulled her over to him, and then snuggled into his chest. With his left arm he felt across the seat to where his revolver was hidden. By digging his fingers deep into the crevice between the seat and the wall he could just touch it. It had settled further down with the jouncing of the train.

But it was no good to him. At least he could hide the little five-shot in Carol Ann's handbag under his hat. He might not hurt anyone with it, but he could at least get off the train and in among the soldiers with it. Maybe, he thought, if he could kill one with a few rapid shots in the ear, get his rifle away from him, and then take cover, he might be able to force the others to surrender.

Except Meadows would still have the passengers.

He sighed and put his head back and tried to quiet his mind. He needed sleep and he needed food. And they were both nearly as hard to come by as a plan. He was just going to have to find every opportunity he could to talk with Meadows and keep looking for weaknesses. The one thing that worried him was that he did not believe the railroads were going to surrender any such sum of money. What he figured was going to happen was there was going to be an all-out cavalry attack on the train and the hell with the civilians. He reckoned the army had already taken the matter over and they were not about to be dictated to by any bunch of deserters. Besides, they would reason that Meadows would have no reason to keep the civilians alive once he got the money, so why take a chance with that kind of a ransom?

He shook his head in the darkness of the coach. He could not find a single bright lining in the dark cloud that seemed to have descended. He'd told Molly he was going on a working holiday. Some holiday. He should have stayed with her for a couple of weeks and then told Billy Vail some cock-and-bull story about searching every square mile of the arid western plains for James Meadows and men. Anything Billy Vail might have done to him for such an outrageous lie would have been nothing to the mess he now found himself in.

They were rousted out and lined up against the side of the coaches as soon as it was good light. Only Longarm was ordered out in front. Trooper Sims and Trooper Hanks were at the telegraph table. The rest of the troopers were ranged in such a way that their rifles enfiladed the entire line of passengers. By now the travelers were showing the effects of fear, deprivation, and lack of water, and uncertainty. The boy in his teens—Longarm guessed him to be about fourteen—was visibly sniffling, obviously expecting to be shot at any moment. His mother, a round woman whose face showed the years of living in such a harsh land, was unsuccessfully trying to shut him up lest he call attention to himself.

Lieutenant Meadows, as he styled himself, had placed himself about fifteen yards in front of the passengers. He said, "Attention! I require your attention for an announcement."

The murmuring and shuffling stilled as the crowd grew attentive to what he was going to say.

"It is my sad duty to report to you that the railroad, the very railroad company you gave your money to in return for safe passage, has seen fit to write you off as so much spoiled milk. Last night, or I should say early this morning, they as much as informed me that they didn't give that for your lives." He snapped his fingers. "I have advised them that I will shoot one of you at six P.M. if the money is not delivered by then. Their answer has been to demand seventy-two hours. Seventy-two hours! I ask you, am I expected to just sit here quietly while they marshal their forces for an attack? I can assure you that more than a few of you will die if they attack in strength and there is a pitched battle. They will send cavalry troops, and the ill-bred scum of the back alleys that they usually recruit will not be able to tell soldier from civilian. You may rest assured that many a stray bullet will find its way into you!" He stopped and looked straight at Longarm. "I have been careful to have one of your own monitoring the telegraphic messages flying back and forth. His name is Custis Long and he is a prominent businessman. Mr. Long, do I not speak the truth when I tell these people that the railroad is being intractable and playing me for a fool?"

Longarm took a step forward. He said, "I can't give you their motives, but I can testify that they are stalling."

"You believe, then, that they should be able to get the money, the gold, together sooner?"

"Being as you are demanding gold, it could delay matters. But yes, I'd say they are dragging their feet."

Meadows turned back to the crowd. "You see? Exactly as I have told you. And from one of your own."

A voice said from the group, "Why won't you take greenbacks? Or at least part of it in greenbacks?"

Meadows stared at him for a moment, and Longarm feared the man was going to catch a rifle butt in the head. He noticed that the man who'd been hit the day before was not among the assembled passengers. He reckoned the man was too badly hurt to come outside.

Meadows snapped his fingers. "All right. I will even go that far." He looked around. "Hanks, go roust Mr. Hatch out of his caboose and let us open up the key and relay our new demand. I will take half the money in greenbacks! And if that is not going the extra mile, I don't know what is."

There was a wait while Hanks fetched the half-awake conductor from his bed in the caboose. He sat down before his table, rubbing his eyes, and took the cover off his telegraph key. Longarm was called forth to witness the proceedings while Meadows dictated his new terms. They were the same with the exception of the paper money. Longarm doubted it was going to have much effect. He rather imagined that the railroad company was in touch with the government and the government was in touch with the several cavalry forts in the vicinity. He had never, for one minute, thought that the railroad would start sending money to save their train or their passengers. Once they set a precedent like that, they might as well get out of the train business because every robber gang in every territory would go in for ransoming trains.

But he stood by and faithfully answered that, yes, he had understood this new offer and, as a member of the passengers, heartily approved of its more benevolent terms.

There was a wait of almost an hour before the railroad answered. Apparently, crisis or not, the officers of the company weren't coming in to work any earlier. The passengers, most of them, had slumped down in the shade of the train. A few had wandered off, looking, Longarm wondered, for who knows what. One went too close to where the troopers had their wagons parked and their horses and mules picketed. He was warned off by a sentry.

Finally the railroad replied, but it was more of the same. They were doing their frantic best to raise the money, but it was still difficult in such a town as Odessa even if Lieutenant Meadows was willing to take part payment in cash. The telegram ended by saying; "All measures being taken this end stop pray you will not act hastily stop still require 72 hours to get funds to you stop"

When the message had been written out for him, Meadows turned and waved the piece of paper. He said to all the passengers, "Take a good look at this. It is your death warrant! You are dismissed. You will be called when you are again needed."

A woman called out, "We've got to have to eat. I've got two chir'ren with me. You've got food. What are we supposed to eat."

Meadows looked at them with disdain. "Each other for all I care. Now disperse!"

Longarm was standing nearby when Meadows came up to him, walking with his arms behind his back. He nodded. "Good morning, Mr. Long. I trust you passed an untroubled night."

Longarm said, "Well, other than the fact I expect to be shot pretty shortly, it wasn't a bad night. I had some company to keep me warm."

Meadows smiled and raised an eyebrow. "Janice?"

Longarm nodded. "I hope that was all right. You seem to have your brand on the other one."

Meadows nodded again. He said, as if he were conferring a favor, "You may have your pleasure with Janice to your fill. I find her a little common for my tastes."

Longarm said, "I take it, sir, that you were born a gentleman. You certainly comport yourself thusly."

Meadows gave him a slight nod. "I was, Mr. Long, into gentry in Baltimore. However, an unfortunate quirk in the

111

sea trade robbed my family of its fortune and cast me adrift to my own devices. I was forced to leave my education far short of my goals. The army was my only recourse to ensure a steady diet, so I applied myself to that service with all dilligence. I believe I have spoken to you about the bitterness I felt to be ordered about by my inferiors in intelligence and breeding."

"Yes," Custis said. "Yes, I believe you touched on that." He smiled slightly. "I do want to mention the promotion you gave me to an upstanding businessman. That may be the first time I ever heard a gambler referred to that way."

Meadows drew himself up. "All business is a gamble. Gambling is a business. I note that you dress well and that your clothes are of good quality. I assume from that that you are a successful gambler. Therefore you are a successful businessman."

Longarm laughed slightly. "I can't argue with your logic, sir." He was aware that he was patronizing the man outrageously. A man of less vanity would have been insulted, but Longarm was testing his theory that Meadows's chief weakness was his pride. He decided to push it a little. "Lieutenant Meadows, would you take it amiss if I expressed an interest in your outfit? I know you are on the run, so to speak, and I'd like to see how you are rigged out. By all accounts you have evaded capture or conflict for several weeks now."

"I'd be most happy to show you." They began walking toward where the wagons and horses were. About halfway there Meadows suddenly began to smile.

Longarm said, "Have I missed something?"

Meadows stopped. "You remarked that we had managed to evade detection for several weeks. Would it surprise you to know that we have not only done that, we've managed to rob a bank in the process?"

Longarm stared at him, trying to look stunned. "I don't believe it."

Meadows nodded, looking pleased. "The Texas National Bank in San Angelo. What do you think of that, sir? Took out a considerable sum. I won't mention how much, but of course, it was not the amount we are expecting here."

Longarm said, "That *is* going some. But isn't Fort Concho in San Angelo? You're not going to tell me you robbed a bank in uniform in the same town that is occupied by a fort!"

Meadows laughed out loud. "Sir, it gets better and better. Would you believe that, at the very instant we were robbing that bank, my corporal was at Fort Concho with a wagon requisitioning supplies using fake orders."

"Lord above!" Longarm said. But to himself he thought that that accounted for the missing man who had not been present during the robbery. He would have never, in a thousand years, thought that he was missing because he was visiting the quartermaster of Fort Concho. He said, "I am amazed, Lieutenant Meadows. Amazed."

They had come up to the little grove of mesquite trees where the two wagons were parked. A trooper was standing guard. Meadows ordered him to pull back one of the covering tarps. He said, "You can see that we are well provisioned. We have cans of cheese, barrels of army biscuits, salted beef, dried beans, slabs of cured bacon, cases of canned fruit and tomatoes. We have plenty of ammunition, both for our personal weapons and the Gatling gun, and we have four fifty-gallon barrels of water for the mules and horses in case we have to make a dry march."

Longarm looked at him sideways. "But I bet you know every water hole within two hundred miles of here."

Meadows smiled modestly. "That would be a fair statement. We very seldom have to resort to our reserves."

Longarm said, "Your livestock certainly looks fat enough, though a blind man can see they are hard as iron."

"They do their work. And we change out the weaker animals. It's not difficult."

Longarm leaned into the opened wagon. "Lieutenant Meadows, let me put an idea to you."

"You have my permission."

"Well, you've got a crowd of folks back there at the train is starting to get a little hungry. I'm not saying you and your troopers couldn't handle them if they got out of line. I'm suggesting it wouldn't cost you much, a bag of beans and a side of bacon, to feed them up. Full folks is contented folks. And contented folks is a whole lot easier to handle."

Meadows had stiffened. He said quietly, "Are you suggesting I need to feed that rabble to maintain control over them?"

Longarm said, "Not at all, Lieutenant. Not at all. But if you have to kill a passel of them you won't have anywhere near as many hostages."

Meadows smiled thinly. "Yes, but the railroad won't know that. They only know what comes over the telegraph wire. And I control that."

Longarm shrugged. "I just thought it might be a gesture of goodwill. Maybe get them mad at the railroad for not doing anything. I think they'd be mighty grateful to you." He was watching his man closely, seeing if this new approach might work.

Meadows thought a moment. "You're suggesting that I feed them as a gesture of kindness?"

"A little kindness can sometimes make a friend out of bad dog."

Meadows said, "You have a point, sir. I thank you for bringing it to my attention." He said to the trooper standing by, "Standish!"

"Sir!"

"Make bacon and beans for the passengers and crew. Double rations. Be generous."

"Yes, sir! Coffee, sir?"

"Standish, there is a limit. The bacon and beans and some biscuits will suffice."

As they turned away Meadows said, "Enlisted men are incredibly stupid. Have you observed that, Mr. Long?"

"Weren't you an enlisted man at one time, Lieutenant?"

"Never at heart, Mr. Long. Never at heart."

As they walked back toward the train Longarm said, "Well, Lieutenant, I reckon you'll have the undying gratitude of them folks on the train for them bacon and beans and biscuits." As he said it he watched the man's face closely to see if he might not have taken the jibe about "undying" too far. But Meadows simply looked smugly satisfied.

He said, "Keep the goodwill of your people, Mr. Long, if it doesn't cost too much. Good commanders know that. They also know the benefit of a touch of fear."

Longarm marveled at the conceit of the man. He simply could not be overpraised. Longarm said, "Well, I reckon there is truth in that, sir."

Meadows said, "Mr. Long, would you care to mess with me at lunch? I assure you we will not be having bacon and beans."

Longarm let a few steps pass as if he were considering the offer. Then he said, "You reckon that would be wise, Lieutenant? I mean, you have set me up as sort of the spokesman for the passengers. Wouldn't that make it look like I was changing sides? I had kind of planned to brag on I was the first one you told about feeding the folks. That would kind of pull down from that, don't you reckon?"

"That's good thinking, Mr. Long. I can see you have a head on your shoulder that can see beyond the next rock.

115

A man has got to have an idea of the future or he will not succeed in the present. Yes, I suppose you are right."

Longarm said, "Tell you what I would appreciate, though."

"What would that be."

Longarm looked over at him. "I'd kind of like to have that caboose to myself for about an hour this afternoon."

Meadows looked at him with the faintest of smiles. "Mr. Long, I do not believe that. I don't believe you want that caboose just to yourself. Am I right?"

Longarm tried to smile guiltily. "Well, I reckon you caught me out there."

"Janice, I assume."

"If it's all right with you."

Meadows said, "Quite all right with me. Were I not so concerned with matters of duty, my mind might run along the same lines. Though, to tell you the truth, I am not too happy with Carol Ann right now."

"What do you, uh, plan to do about her? I can understand she did a great disservice to you."

Meadows said grimly, "We will have to see how this whole affair works out, won't we. No, you have your pleasure with Janice. You know, of course, Mr. Long, she is used goods."

Longarm said, "I understand. And I appreciate you warning me. I'll make sure she cleans herself good."

"Do that. I certainly do."

"Any idea when I might have the caboose?"

"Hatch is going to need a nap. When it is all clear I'll send a trooper around to alert you. You should have your privacy for at least an hour."

"I am much obliged. I think it would be a good idea if you let these folks know you are going to feed them."

"As soon as I check the telegraph for any news."

116

Chapter 7

Carol Ann seemed to be napping when they slipped out of the car after being notified by the trooper that Longarm had permission to use the caboose. It seemed that all Carol Ann did was lay, curled into a ball, as if she was trying to shut the world out. She hadn't even responded to the lunch that had been served. It had been a great success with the passengers, and had caused Meadows to again thank Longarm, if somewhat loftily, for the idea. He'd made it sound like something he would have gotten around to thinking of if his mind was not so involved with matters of greater weight. The communications with the railroad company were not proceeding well, and Longarm was getting worried that Meadows would actually shoot someone. It was clear to him that the railroad company was stalling, that troops were most likely on the way, and that the whole situation could turn nasty without much help from either side. Longarm felt compelled to find some way to stop Meadows and his men, but nothing would come to mind.

As he and Janice walked toward the caboose he took her hand and said awkwardly, "I ain't exactly explained this deal to you because I wasn't at all sure it would come about. I been kind of buddying up with Meadows, trying to figure the sonofabitch out." He cleared his throat. "I, uh, asked him for the use of the caboose for an hour or so for privacy so we could, uh, uh . . ."

She said, "Make love?"

"Well, yeah," he said. "But you ain't got to worry. I mainly wanted to get in there to see if I could find some kind of weapon. Railroad trains, as a rule, carry flares like they have on a ship. If I could get my hands on three or four of those I might could cause them some trouble."

She said, "So I'm your excuse."

They climbed up the steps of the caboose and opened the door. Longarm said, "Well, something like that."

He let them both in, and then slid home a bolt so that the door couldn't be opened except from the inside. There were two bay windows that stuck out on each side so the conductor could see forward the length of the train. But they had curtains, and while he pulled one set, Janice pulled the other.

The caboose was a combination of sleeping quarters and office. There were two bunk beds on either side of the car. At the end was a big rolltop desk. Next to it was a large chest with a hinge and hasp, secured with a big padlock. Over the desk was a big cabinet that wasn't locked. Longarm started looking through the middle drawer of the desk for the key to the big chest. He said, "I'm looking for anything, but mainly I'm looking for those distress rockets or flares or whatever you call them. You know, the kind that ships fire off when they are sinking. I've heard that trains carry the same thing, though I can't think for what. If a train was to break down out here, that flare would have to go up about ten miles for anyone to be able to see it. But railroads like to have all the latest things. I reckon they don't want to be able to have folks say they ain't up on their emergency procedures."

She said, "There's a crowbar in the corner. Why don't you just break off the lock with that?"

"Because I ain't ready to call attention to myself. The key ought to be in here someplace if the conductor ain't got it."

She was standing behind him. "What about those overhead cabinets? Wouldn't they maybe have something?"

"Them flares are the kind of thing they would keep under lock and key." He was still rummaging around in the desk, not looking at her. He could hear the rustle of clothes, but he thought she was either sitting down or stooping to look under the bunk beds. He said, "Janice, I'm going to trust you to tell you something. I noticed you left Carol Ann's bag laying on our seat. Is that little pistol still in it?"

She said, "Oh, Lord! Yes. I never thought. But I don't think Carol Ann is ever going to move again. I can't even get her to talk to me."

Longarm said, "Well, what I was going to trust you about was that I didn't care if she had that gun back or not. Can she shoot?"

"I don't know."

Longarm said, "She might just provide the distraction I need. I . . ." He broke off as he found a key that was labeled as the same make as the padlock. "Here we are. I bet this does the trick." He moved to his right and inserted the key and turned it. The U of the padlock popped out of the lock. He took it out of the hasp and raised the lid. There, in a tray, was a big flare gun that looked like a pistol but was about the size of two of them. There were at least six flares with it, cartridges about one and a half times the size of a 12 shotgun shell. They fired a sort of phosphorus shell that Longarm knew would nearly burn metal. They were not toys. He carefully picked up the flare gun and broke it open as you would a shotgun you were about to load.

The diameter of the bore was about an inch. Longarm had seen them fired and he estimated their range at about two hundred yards. He said, "Janice, look at this. If we can't do some good with a weapon like this we can't do no good at all. I—" He was turning as he spoke to show her the flare gun. He had turned all the way around when he saw her. He said, "Oh, Lord! Oh, my Lord!"

She was standing there with nothing on but her sheer silk stockings held up by gaily colored garters. His mouth dropped open. She was as perfectly formed as any woman he'd ever seen, from her small, uptilted breasts with their large nipples, to the flare of her hips, from her tiny waist down to her straight, shapely legs.

But what took his eye the quickest was the auburn red of her bush that was set off so startlingly from her creamy skin. He said, "You are a redhead! Why is your hair blond?" Even as he said it he realized it was not a very smart thing to say to a woman who was standing before him naked.

She said, "Oh, I dyed my hair as an experiment. It excites some men when they find out my hair is really auburn."

"Lordy," he said huskily. He could smell the musk of her from the few feet that separated them. He said shakily, "Janice, I didn't really mean . . ."

She said, "Why not? Why should we pass up this chance?" She moved toward him, and slowly went down on her knees and began unbuttoning his jeans. When his pants were open she put her hand inside and took out his member. For a moment she caressed it with her fingertips, looking up into his eyes. Then, ever so gently, she slid it into her mouth. He groaned, feeling his legs go weak. For a moment she undulated her mouth and tongue around him, and then she stood up and lay down on one of the beds, lying on her back with her legs open so that he could see. With one finger she gently began caressing herself. She said softly, "Take

120

off your clothes, honey. I'll be ready for you by then."

When he was undressed, he went to her and lowered himself as she enveloped him with her arms and her legs. She was such a tiny thing, much smaller than she'd looked with her clothes on, that he feared his weight would be too much for her. He did not know how he entered her. It was not done by his hand and both of hers were around his neck. It seemed as if her vagina simply reached out and sucked him in.

She was so warm and slick, he thought for a second he would not be able to hold himself. But then he frantically cast his mind to everything he could think of that would delay him. But her mouth was fastened to his and the muscles inside her vagina were squeezing his member and then releasing it, massaging it as no other woman had ever done. He began to stroke into her as her hips moved in perfect rhythm with his. For a moment he thought he could last, but then she moved her mouth from his and gently began to lick his ear. With a mighty convulsion he ejaculated, feeling himself spurt into her with such force he could feel himself emptying out.

He went immediately limp. She kept him clutched to her with her arms and legs, slowly moving her hips to bring him down easy. He was gasping for breath, spent. "Oh, my," he said. "Oh, my. My, my, my. Never like that."

She used her hands to lift his head so she could kiss him all over his face and neck. She said softly in his ear, "Was that good, baby? Did you like that?"

His strength was still so spent all he could do was lie on her limply. He said, "Oh, oh, oh. I have never felt it like that. Never. Oh, I don't ever want to come again. I don't think I'll ever need to come again. I'm empty."

After a while he sat up. His strength was returning, but he was still unsteady. He turned his head to look at her as she lay back on the bed. He said, "You may have the best body I have ever seen. Hell, you may have the best body ever made. I don't think I could ever get enough of you."

She stretched her arms over her head, a move that made her breasts stand out prominently. "We don't have to stop with one."

He said, "Oh, Janice, darlin' . . . Ain't nothing I'd rather do than what we just did. But I've got to see what else I can find and figure out a way to get those flares back to our coach."

She said, "I can help with that. There's a lot of room under my skirt and petticoats. I can hide them and keep them for you."

He frowned. "That's a shade dangerous. You get caught with something like that, I don't know where Meadows would stop. Listen, you know that bastard better than I do. Is he really going to kill someone at six this evening or is he just going to telegraph that he did?"

She shook her head hard from side to side. "Oh, no. If he has said he is going to kill someone he will do it. Custis, I guess I can call you that now . . . Custis, he is the meanest man I have ever known. He used to make Carol Ann watch while he did it to some of the other girls."

"Yeah, but that ain't killing a man in cold blood."

"He's done that. He got into an argument with a man at Carol Ann's house. Not where she lives, but her place of business. They were arguing at the bar. Neither one had a gun because it is a house rule that all the gentlemen must check their firearms at the door. James left and came back five minutes later and shot the man dead. There was one witness besides the girls who work there, so he shot him too. We had a hell of a time getting those bodies out of the house and into the Potomac River. Oh, no. Don't think that James Meadows is not capable of anything. What makes him so dangerous is that he never gets angry, so you are never expecting his worst until it happens."

Longarm got dressed, thinking about what Janice had said. He spent some time rummaging through the bottom of the chest and then the cabinet. All he found besides the flare gun and six cartridges were four torpedoes like the type Meadows had used to stop the train. They were about half the size of a stick of dynamite, but flat on one side so they'd stay in place as the train ran over them and detonated them with its weight. They would be hard to ignite, but they did contain blasting powder.

Longarm said, "Janice, I've still got a pistol. It's hid at the end of my seat, shoved down by the cushion."

"I know," she said. "I noticed it this morning. It was working its way up so I pushed it down further."

Longarm said, "But I only got the six cartridges that are in the cylinder. They took the rest of my ammunition. Six cartridges and there are eight of them. And you can't always count on killing a man with one shot." He thought a moment. Then he shook his head. "I been in some tight spots before, but this is about the tightest."

"I would imagine you have been, gambling and all."

He had trusted her with everything else, so he saw no point in keeping a final truth from her. He reached in his pocket and took out his star. He said, "I'm not a gambler, Janice, I'm a deputy United States marshal."

She looked at the badge, her eyes getting big. "Oh, my goodness! Who'd have ever thought it. Why, that just makes me feel ever so much safer. You a federal marshal. I reckon you are the first one of those I ever made love with. My!"

He said, "You understand that this has to be our secret. If Meadows knew who I was, he'd feel threatened and probably have me shot. I mean you can't even tell Carol Ann. Especially Carol Ann."

She said, "I don't even know Carol Ann anymore. She acts like a dead person already. I'm not so sure she's not as crazy as James Meadows." She reached up and touched his cheek. "Honey, I am on your side. I won't say a word about anything. Besides, I'll be carrying those flares. That makes me a part of it."

He said, looking away from her face, "That little trick you do inside of you, that squeezing and then letting go with some muscles I didn't even know women had. Do you do that with all the men?"

She smiled, put her hand on the back of his neck, and pulled his head down and kissed him. "Honey, I did that for love. I've been the way I was with very few men. And none lately. You are quite a handsome man, Mr. Long. I had eyes for you the first moment I saw you."

He cleared his throat. "Uh, well, we better go to figuring out how to get this stuff back to our car. I've found some twine. You reckon we could tie that flare gun on the inside of your leg, your thigh?"

"Oh, my, yes. And we can put the cartridges in my garters."

"It might be uncomfortable."

"But not for long. As soon as we get back to the car I can find a place to hide them."

Longarm said, "I can put the torpedoes in my boots. Janice, I hate for you to be taking this kind of risk."

She was standing next to him in her chemise, waiting for him to tie the flare gun to the inside of her thigh with the twine. She said in a low voice, "Mr. Long, I am deeply ashamed of my part in this. It seems the least I can do to try and undo some of the harm I helped cause."

He looked at her, wanting to put some questions to her, but his heart was not in it. Instead he said, musing, "I can kill James Meadows. That won't be no trick at all. The hard part is figuring out what those seven troopers will do. They could cause a hell of a lot of damage among the live bodies on this train with those Springfield rifles. What do you think, are they loyal to Meadows?"

She shrugged. "I don't know, Mr. Long. They do obey him promptly. And they do look to him for guidance."

"Yeah," Longarm said, "they do. And there is no telling what they might do if I cut down their leader. He's been taking pretty good care of them. You know they robbed a bank, didn't you?"

"Robbed a bank! Besides deserting, when did they find time to do that?"

Longarm laughed slightly. "It wasn't a big robbery. But it was enough to provision and outfit them. This was to be the big payday. This is what all the desertion and other crimes has been about. The hundred and fifty thousand dollars. That's a fair amount of money to men who have been making fourteen dollars a month plus room and board and the worst horses the army can buy."

She said, "I just feel terrible. I can't even say I didn't know. I wish I could. But Custis, you have got to believe me that I didn't know matters were going to come to this. It was not explained that way to Carol Ann and me. At least not to me."

Longarm said gently, "Let's get you rigged out and dressed. You can tell me the details as we go along. I'm going to have to tie this flare gun kind of tight with this twine. But I will secure it with bow knots so you can just pull them loose and have it ready to hand when we get ready to use it."

"I don't care," she said. She was putting on her bodice while Longarm knelt by her shapely legs, laid the flare gun on the inside of her soft thigh, and began winding twine around it. She said, "All I was supposed to do was get the information out of that major about when the payroll would be shipped and on what train. That part was easy. I didn't feel as if we were stealing from anybody. You understand what I mean?"

"Yes. It was the government. It wasn't like it was someone you knew."

"Yes," she said in a shamed voice. "Of course I know now that it was wrong. I can only plead that James can be a very persuasive talker when he wants to be. He swore to us that no one would be hurt. He said they would stop the train, open the mail car, take the payroll, and ride away. Carol and I were to go on to Alpine and put up at a certain boardinghouse and wait there for word from him. When it came she would go to him—I think he expected to go to California—and then I would be free to return."

"What was your reward?"

She looked even more ashamed. "The house. I was to be the madam, to take Carol's place. Mr. Long, it was a gold mine. I knew I could make enough money in a very short time to set myself up as a lady somewhere else. I was going to make changes, have the girls pay in more than they had been." She looked away and sighed. "I was greedy. I had to be to be foolish enough to trust James Meadows."

"What about Carol Ann?"

"Her? She would have helped him rob that bank. She was that gone on him."

"There," Longarm said. He stood up and inspected his work. "That ought to do. That flare gun is tight as Billy's Vail's hatband and them cartridges are fine in your garter belts. Bad as I hate to say it, I reckon you can put your skirt back on now. We better be for getting out of here, before someone comes looking. I'll just put things back like I found them. Hopefully Hatch won't notice the missing flares, and if he does, won't be so damn dumb as to tell Meadows."

126

She stopped him just before he could open the caboose door. With her hand on his chest she said, "Custis, do you think we have a chance? Perhaps I am not showing it, but I am afraid. I'm probably more afraid than anyone because I know James Meadows. So does Carol Ann, but she has simply retreated into herself. Tell me, please, that you think you can stop him."

Longarm made a face. "Janice, I ain't exactly got the cool, calm confidence of a Christian with four aces, but I got hope. I *think* I been in tighter places than this, but for the life of me, I can't remember any. Let's just play out our string and see what happens."

As they were walking back to their coach at the far end of the train, walking on the west side so as to be out of sight of the troopers and the few passengers who used the east side for shade or to just sit outside, Longarm said, "You reckon Meadows can be talked out of this foolishness?"

"What do you mean?"

"I mean just go up to him and point out the futility of his project. That railroad ain't any more going to give him a hundred and fifty thousand dollars than I'm likely to give him ten to get him to sing a gospel song."

She said, "I don't think you can talk James out of anything. It's Carol Ann I'm worried about if he doesn't get his way. He will do something horrible to her. He won't just kill her."

Longarm eyed her out of the corner of his vision. "How are you doing with all that hardware in there between your legs?"

"It rubs a little," she said. "But it won't be any trouble the rest of the way. It's not far now."

He said, "I wish I was where that flare pistol was. These torpedoes in my boots are starting to get right uncomfortable."

She said, "Just don't limp."

He smiled. "Ain't much chance of that. Janice, once we get you unloaded, I want you to forget you ever did this. Don't even tell Carol Ann."

She said, "I would as soon tell James Meadows as tell her. It would practically be the same."

"Are you angry at her for getting you into this?"

She shook her head with a quick, jerky motion. "Not angry, just disappointed. Though I don't know why. Ordinarily Carol Ann is one of the most capable women I have ever known. But anytime anything involves James she just seems to go to pieces. I guess I should have expected it." She sighed. "Besides, I was doing wrong myself and knew it." She suddenly looked around at him. "I just remembered that you a federal marshal. What I did is a crime, isn't it? Getting that information from that major and telling James."

He said, "I don't know what you are talking about. I haven't heard a word you've said since I turned around and you were standing there without your clothes on. A sight like that will make a man deaf and dumb."

"You trust me, then?"

"Of course I trust you. I wouldn't have asked for your help if I didn't trust you."

But he did not tell her, nor had he told her, nor was he going to tell her, that his assignment had been James Meadows and anyone with him. And she was part of that description. Longarm did not consider himself a particularly close-mouthed man, but he made it a habit to never tell anyone more than they needed to know. The unsaid word never had to be retracted. It was a practice that was almost second nature to him. It gave him the appearance of being open and friendly, while at the same time he was keeping his own counsel except when he could profit by releasing information. And he saw no good reason for Janice to know that he had been on to her and Carol Ann even before James Meadows had stopped the train.

They boarded the train and she slid into his seat. He stood in the aisle, guarding her from view while she took the flare gun and the flare cartridges out from under her skirt.

Carol Ann didn't seem to have moved. To Longarm's eye she looked like a lanky baby curled up in her crib sucking her thumb. It seemed that she hadn't moved for hours. He'd have thought her bladder would have roused her.

There were only three people on the car: the injured man and two women who were sitting with him and trying to comfort him. He'd stopped moaning and groaning, and was now just making little muttering sounds every now and then.

Behind Longarm Janice said softly, "It's all right."

He turned around. She was smoothing her skirt down. She said, "There was room at the end of the cushion. I just shoved them down in there. The flare thing is at the back toward the back cushion. The cartridges are kind of lined up."

"What about my revolver? You didn't bury it under all that, did you?"

She shook her head. "No. It's on top. You can reach it easy."

"I'm going forward here," he said. "See about this man."

He walked to the end of the coach where the two women had the injured man stretched out on one of the seats. They were keeping a wet cloth on his forehead and one of them was holding his hand. They'd rigged a sort of makeshift bandage around his head, and Longarm could see a splotch at the crotch of the man's pants. He said, "He doing poorly, ladies?"

The elderly woman who was freshening the cloth said, "I don't see no chance fer him. He's a gone 'un sure as I'm born."

The other lady said, "He can't talk anymore and can barely walk. And he's wet himself. I wish that devil of a soldier had just killed him. He would have counted it a blessing, I'm sure."

Longarm looked down at the stout middle-aged man who'd run into a taste of a country he should never have set foot in. Longarm took him for a banker or salesman from back East. Maybe he'd thought it was time to bring enlightenment to the ladies of the West with a new line of corsets. Whatever his mission had been, he'd have been better off staying in his own kind of country.

Longarm walked slowly back to his seat and sat down. He leaned his head forward. He said, "As a lawman I've run into some real low-down snakes and varmints. But I believe I despise this Meadows worse than any I have ever come across. And what makes it so bad is I can't tell the bastard because I've got to keep jollying him until I can make my play. If he ends up in my hands when this is over, he is going to wish he had never drawn breath." Longarm turned his head and looked at Janice. "Do you understand what I mean by that?"

She gave a little shiver. "Please don't get that tone in your voice. Even though you don't mean me, it scares me to death."

He hit himself on the thigh. "You can't know how hard it is for me to keep on pretending with that arrogant bastard. But I have to. I have to make him think I think he is the cock of the walk. I've got to keep him off balance." He paused for a moment. "Until my moment comes. Then we'll see."

Janice glanced out the window. "He looks pleased enough with himself. Look at him standing there—the king surveying his domain."

Longarm leaned over and looked past her shoulder. Meadows was standing with his back to them in the middle of what

130

Longarm had come to think of as the parade ground. It was the area where the passengers were assembled, and it had been tramped over by troops and civilians alike so that most of its rough spots had been smoothed out by shoe leather. Meadows had his gauntleted gloved hands clasped behind him as he stood there slowly turning his head from left to right and then back to center again.

Longarm stood up. "I reckon I better go see what the great man has to say. Maybe some new developments have occurred. You do know that I am considered the liaison with the passengers."

"Was that his idea?"

Longarm said grimly, "It sure as hell wasn't mine."

He stepped down from the train and walked slowly toward Meadows, whistling lowly as he went so as not to startle the man. Meadows turned as Longarm got within a few yards. "Ah, Mr. Long. I trust you have had a most satisfactory tryst."

Longarm smiled the smile he could summon up even when it hurt him. "Well, I reckon you could say that. She trysted this way and that, but I managed to stay up with her."

Meadows chuckled. "You have a fine sense of humor, Mr. Long. A good quality in times as trying as these."

"Maybe a little of the same medicine would be good for you, Lieutenant. That Miss Carol Ann looks a little down in the mouth. You might ought to cheer her up with a little of that caboose juice."

The smile left Meadows's face. "The woman has got some matters to answer for. I do not reward stupidity or neglect or disobedience of orders."

Longarm said, "What do you hear from the railroad?"

"The same, Mr. Long. Delay, delay, delay. They must think I'm a fool. Well, when I shoot a passenger in"—he got out his watch and looked at it—"in a little less than three hours, I believe they will have second thoughts."

Longarm cleared his throat and looked down at the ground as if he were acting deferential. "Lieutenant, you reckon it will do all that much good to shoot one of these birds? I mean, they might not actually believe you done it."

"The conductor will tell them."

"Yeah, but they might just figure you had a gun to his head and was making him send whatever you told him."

The ex-lieutenant fixed Longarm with a hard eye. "Mr. Long, I don't believe you understand human nature to the same degree that I do. The message that the conductor sends will be quite different if he has just seen me carry out my vow by shooting one of the passengers."

"Over a telegraph?"

"Yes. I know you find that hard to believe, but his very touch on that key will be changed by what he has seen."

Longarm made a little motion with his hand. "It wouldn't be the same as if you just told him you'd shot a passenger?"

"No. He will transmit his emotions through his hand. You may depend on it. Human nature, Mr. Long, is my study. I fancy myself fairly expert at it."

"I see," Longarm said slowly. But he was thinking that the man was crazier than he'd given him credit for. He was, Longarm believed, truly out of touch with reality.

Yet for all of that, he still felt he had to make one last attempt to get Meadows to see reason. He said, "Lieutenant, would you mind if I offered a few comments? Strictly in your best interests, sir?"

Meadows had been looking off into the distance. He brought his gaze back to Longarm. "Mr. Long, let it always be said about me that I welcomed advice from intelligent men. Speak your piece, Mr. Long."

Longarm stirred a little dust with his boot toe. "Well, sir, I don't know if this is true or not for all gamblers, but I think it has stood them as wins in the long run in good stead. Sometimes, Lieutenant, you get dealt a hand that you can't win with no matter how well you play it. What I'm trying to say, sir, is that sometimes you got to know when to pitch a hand in. Ain't no good ever come of throwing good money after bad."

"And you think that is what I am doing in my persistence in demanding the railroad pay me the money they owe me?"

"Yessir, I do. And I'll tell you why."

"Pray do."

"Lieutenant, I think they are just stringing you along. I don't think they got any more intention of paying you that money than a goat does of keeping his word."

Meadows looked grim. "Then they will find out to their sorrow that my vow will be kept. They will find corpses, Mr. Long, corpses."

"Some of them corpses, Lieutenant, might be some of your troopers."

"I can accept casualties, Mr. Long. Any commander must learn to do so."

"Well, sir, what I'm getting at is what you might call a strategic withdrawal until you can improve your chances. Hell, like I told you before, this ain't the only train in the world. But this is one bad piece of ground to try and defend." He pointed south, down the tracks. "It would be my guess that you have troops from Fort Concho and Fort Davis even now on their way by rail." He pointed north. "And I would reckon you got a hell of a posse of lawmen and a mixed bag of civilians coming from Odessa by train. And both of them getting closer and closer by the hour." He pointed vaguely to the east. "I ain't exactly sure of my directions or my distances, but I would reckon Fort Stockton ain't much more than seventy or eighty miles by horseback yonder. And you know they have got the word by now. I'd reckon they are on the march even as we stand here."

Meadows said, "I agree with every word you have said."

Earnestly, Longarm said, "Sir, you have a clean line of retreat to the west. There is nothing between you and the New Mexico Territory except a light breeze."

"I do not retreat, Mr. Long." He said it stiffly. "That is not a line of suggestion an intelligent man would make."

"All right," Longarm said doggedly, "then a strategic withdrawal so that you can keep your troops intact and not take any unnecessary losses. Lieutenant, you are sitting here and you are diminishing your supplies and your provisions. And the longer you sit here, the less supplies you are going to have to make a withdrawal to the west. Take what you can from these people and then leave! Go! Let the army expend all the effort it can, only to arrive and find their will-o'-the-wisp vanished! You'll be a hero to these people. As brave a military commander as you does not sacrifice civilians."

Meadows turned cold eyes on him. "They are not civilians, Mr. Long. They are strategic hostages. I have no more feeling for them than I would if they were already corpses."

The torpedoes had worked their way down further into Longarm's boots. He wasn't sure he'd be able to walk naturally. He said, "All right, let's forget about them. But you are about to be descended on from three sides by superior forces. Is that good tactics? Aren't you staying in a pocket where you'll have hell extricating yourself?"

Meadows suddenly smiled, and that light gleamed in his eye that Longarm had first noticed. "Is it a pocket, Mr. Long, or a trap? I have the Gatling. It is flat terrain with no cover. They will pay in blood for every step they advance."

Longarm shrugged. "Well, thank you for listening to me. I ought not to have been sounding off. After all, you're the soldier, not me."

"It is good of you to note that, Mr. Long. I know you spoke in the best interests of myself and my men."

Longarm ran his tongue over his lips. "Lieutenant, I've got a craving for something sweet. I noticed you had some cans of peaches in your wagons over yonder. Would you greatly mind if I helped myself to a can?"

Meadows said, "Not at all, Mr. Long. You have earned privileges. But I'd like you back at the telegraph table fairly quickly. I will be sending them a final warning and I would like you there to hear their answer. You will be my chief witness, Mr. Long, of how fair and long-suffering and tolerant I have been."

"Yessir," Longarm said. "I'll just slip over there to the wagons and get me that can of peaches and be right on back."

"Tell the trooper on duty you have my permission. If he does not believe you, have him look my way and I'll signal with a wave of my arm."

"I am much obliged, Lieutenant. Sometimes I swear I'm worse than a child about sweets."

He gave the lieutenant a little half salute and then started for the wagons, some two hundred yards distance. The torpedoes were rubbing painfully against his ankles, but he willed himself to walk naturally, not sauntering, but not seeming to hurry either.

He came finally into the sparse shade of the mesquite clump where the wagons were partially protected. As he stepped close to the first wagon the guard came instantly toward him and said, "Halt!"

Longarm said, moving closer to the wagon, "Hold on there, Trooper. The lieutenant said I could have a can of peaches. Step out there in the clear and he'll signal to you."

"Lieutenant Meadows said you could?"

"Yes. But you are supposed to get a signal. I'd step out there if I was you."

He was standing right by the wagon furthest from the train. The tarpaulin was still back as they'd left it earlier. As the trooper stepped out into the clear to receive the wave from Meadows, Longarm stooped quickly and took two of the torpedoes out of his right boot. With a swift motion he broke them in two, spilling a little of the blasting powder they contained. He shoved them in between some sacks of dried beans. He heard the trooper coming back and he turned quickly for the other wagon, pulling the tarpaulin back as he did. He said, "Nope, no peaches in there."

The trooper said, "Lootenant said it wuz all raight, but you be quick 'bout it. I doan know 'bout you civilians messin' round military supplies."

Longarm got himself on the other side of the wagon from the trooper. He already had the last two torpedoes in his hand. He pulled the canvas back at the end and made a show of looking around while he broke the torpedoes and shoved them in between two wooden casks of blasting powder. He said cheerfully, "Ain't back here neither."

"Hell an' damnation!" the trooper said. "I never seed a man heve so much trouble findin' a can 'o peaches." He jerked the canvas back halfway down the first wagon, stuck in his hand, and flipped Longarm a can of the fruit.

Longarm caught it in the air. "Wonder how I missed that."

"Blind, I reckon," the trooper said disgustedly. He went around both wagons pulling the canvas back in place. "Just don't be figgerin' you kin make yoreself free with gummit supplies."

Longarm took out his small pocketknife and punched a hole in the top of the can. As he sauntered toward where Hatch was sitting at the telegraph table, he threw his head back and sucked the juice out of the peaches. After nothing but the gyppy water it tasted incredibly good and sweet.

Meadows's telegrapher, Hanks, was nowhere in sight. And Meadows himself seemed to have disappeared. Longarm supposed he was in his headquarters in the caboose planning his next message to the railroad company.

Hatch was sitting with his head in his hands. He looked up as Longarm approached. He had put aside his conductor's cap and his hair was thin and graying. Longarm thought that he had aged a good ten years since their ordeal had began.

He said, "Mr. Hatch, how are you holding up?"

"Not well, Mr. Long. Not well." His voice was weak and thready. "I am at my wits' end. I have had my train stolen and now all my passengers are at the mercy of a madman. I don't know what to do."

"What he tells you, Mr. Hatch. That's all any of us can do unless we want a bullet in the brain."

Hatch put his hands to the sides of his head. "I almost think I'd welcome it, Mr. Long. Welcome it and be done with the whole mess."

"I take it the news is not good from the railroad company."

Hatch looked back up at him. "Mr. Long, that railroad company ain't goin' to send no money an' anybody but a fool would know it. Railroad companies don't give in to robbers. They did, pretty soon they'd be out of bid'ness. All they are doin' is stallin', stallin' till they can get some army troops here. Or some sheriffs' posses."

"You get that sense of it from their messages?"

"Hell, I get that sense of it right out of my own head. I been a good many years around these big companies. They

137

ain't scared of that fancy soldier over there, no matter how much he thinks of hisself. I'll tell you what is gonna happen, Mr. Long. Armies is gonna arrive from ever' direction and we is gonna be right square in the middle of a pitched battle. And the ones is kilt first will be the lucky ones. I'll tell you that fer nothin'."

Longarm glanced up to see Meadows and Hanks making their way toward the telegraph table. "Well, Mr. Hatch, I think we are about to decide somebody's life here and now. Is there any way you can fake the return message to make it sound more favorable? As if they are getting close with the money?"

Hatch shook his head sorrowfully. "I know what you be after, Mr. Long, and I would have done some such long ago if I figgered I could git away with it, but that telegrapher Meadows has got with him knows his stuff. I tried to fool him on somethin' didn't amount to much, but he set me straight right quick."

"No chance then? I fear he is going to shoot a passenger at six P.M. if we can't head him off."

Hatch said, looking tired and old, "We can't with this machine. If they'd sound a little more helpful on the other end I might could work it around, but all they do is keep astin' fer more time. And that ain't foolin' nobody, much less Meadows."

Longarm said, "Well, get ready. Here they are."

Chapter 8

There were three transmissions each way as Meadows continued to hammer for payment and the railroad company continued to plead for time. The messages from the railroad company showed a conciliatory tone, a willingness to compromise, while Meadows's return wires became increasingly more threatening and demanding. He finished his last message with: "You now have forty-five minutes until the deadline. I will proceed unless assured the money is en route. End of message."

Hatch let the key go dead and slowly closed the cover and hung his head. He said to Meadows, "Lieutenant, by now the company knows that I am here and witnessing all the proceedings. Couldn't you let yore man do the actual key work? I am plumb give out. I am too old for this sort of jumpin' about."

Meadows said, "We shall see. I cannot promise you anything at this point." He took out his watch. "Less than a quarter of an hour." He said to the trooper standing by, "Hanks!"

"Sir!"

"My compliments to Corporal Cupper and he is to have

all passengers fall out and assemble along the west side of the train."

The trooper saluted. He started off and then hesitated. "Would that include that feller with the cracked head?"

Meadows fixed him with a look. "Trooper Hanks, did you hear me make any exceptions?"

"Nosir. I jus' thought seein' he—"

"Trooper!"

"Sir!"

"Don't think, Trooper Hanks. Obey. Do you understand?"

"Yessir!"

"Then go and carry out my orders."

Meadows shook his head. "They are getting more and more lax every day. They need a good dose of close-order drill. Perhaps I'll have Corporal Cupper put them through their paces after the execution formation."

Longarm said, "Lieutenant, surely you are not going to go through with this. This execution as you call it."

Meadows turned his head slowly and regarded Longarm. "You heard me say it, didn't you?"

"Yes. Yes, I did. But, to tell you the truth, I had hoped that that was only for the railroad company."

"A bluff?"

Longarm shrugged. "You might call it that."

Meadows smiled without humor. "You will find, Mr. Long, that I never bluff. You and Mr. Hatch might as well come along now. You will be required to watch the execution so that your reactions may be forwarded to the railroad company."

Hatch said, "I don't want to go. You can't make me watch no execution as you call it." He stood up, and there was determination in his tired old face. "It's murder is what I call it an' I ain't gonna watch."

Meadows said simply, "You can watch or you can be the

victim. I will leave it to your choice. In fact I think it will make an even stronger impression on the railroad company if I shoot one of their employees." He said it all quietly, calmly, as if he were discussing the weather or the price of horse feed.

Hatch sat back down, dropping onto his folding canvas stool as if his legs had given out. He said, his voice weak, "That is uncommon cruel, sir. You ruin me with my company by taking my train, you ruin my reputation, and now you insist I be a part of yore depredations by bearing witness."

Meadows said, in a voice that was not unkind, "It is for the very emotion that you just displayed that I want your presence at the execution. No, don't call it that. Let us call it an example of my determination that your company should know that I am serious."

Hatch's faced suddenly flushed. "My God, man, that there is a telegraph! They cain't hear me an' see me! What do you reckon? It's a blamed copper wire sendin' out little electric signals. They ain't got no feelin's! Copper wire don't feel nothin'!"

Meadows smiled. "I believe it will come across, Mr. Hatch. Isn't it said that every operator has a certain touch?"

"I guess so. So what?"

"I think yours will be different after you witness this example of how serious I am." He looked at his watch. "We had better start walking that way, gentlemen. The time is growing nigh." To Hatch he said, "Be assured, sir, I take no personal pleasure in this. I am a military officer and I am simply executing a military maneuver to achieve a goal."

Hatch said, mumbling, "By killin' a poor civilian ain't got nothin' to defend himself with."

Longarm trailed along behind the other two as they descended the slight slope toward the train. The engine and coaches had come to seem lifeless, like a deserted house or an old barn in ruins. Longarm had a hard time envisioning the train as a moving, noisemaking object that had once been going about the business of taking people from one place to another. Now it just sat there, lifeless, its boiler cold, its firebox full of dead ashes.

As he walked he thought of who and what he was. He was a duly constituted officer of the law, a federal officer, and even though it might not be the wisest move in the long run, he did not believe that he could stand by and watch an innocent civilian shot down while he had the means to prevent it. It might only be a temporary delay, but he felt he could not in good conscience refuse to make any attempt to stop such an act. The derringer was under his belt buckle, two .38-caliber bullets ready to fire. And there was the thin stiletto in his boot. And there were his fists. As long as he was armed it was his responsibility to stop a murder by any means that came to hand.

He was well aware that it would most probably mean his own death, and might not in the end delay proceedings for more than a few minutes. But all of that did not count. He would have to act. He would wait and hope that Meadows was bluffing, but when the moment came that he, Longarm, realized that the man was going through with it, he would have to step in and take a hand.

Even if it cost him his life. But if it did, he would at least have the satisfaction of knowing that James Meadows would leave the earth before himself.

With the decision made he felt lighter and calmer. The matter was now out of his hands. Events would dictate his actions.

The passengers had nearly emptied out of the coaches by the time they arrived. Meadows halted some twenty yards back from the coaches. Longarm watched as Carol Ann and

Janice were the last out the forward door of their coach. Janice tried to help her companion down, but Carol Ann shook off her arm and marched, shoulders slumped, handbag clutched in her hand, down the line to her place against the coach.

The last passengers off were the two women helping the man with the concussion. They were practically carrying him, and two men came from the crowd to lend a hand. The man walked as if he couldn't see. The elk's tooth had come out of his vest pocket and swung loose on its gold chain, moving jerkily with his faltering steps.

Corporal Cupper came up to Meadows, came to attention, and saluted. "Passengers assembled, sir. All present and accounted for, sir!"

Meadows said, "Very good, Corporal. Choose a four-man firing squad. You will be in command. Leave one sentry on top of the train and the sentry at the wagons. The other four will form the squad."

"Yessir!"

Meadows raised his arm and pointed at the little knot of people near the middle of the line of passengers. "Arrest the man with the wounded head. Conduct him to the end of the caboose and stand him in place. Form your squad first, of course."

Cupper saluted. "Yessir!" He wheeled, barking orders to the other troopers. Four quickly formed into a two-abreast squad, marching in step under his orders.

Hatch said, "My God, man, have you no feelin's atall? Ain't it enough you've cracked his skull? You gonna kill him also?"

Meadows looked around at him coolly. "The man is going to die anyway, Mr. Hatch. I have looked at him myself. I am doing him a kindness by cutting short his sufferings."

Hatch muttered something, looking away as he said it.

Meadows said sharply, "What did you say, Mr. Hatch?"

"I was just wondering to myself, if you don't mind."

"And what were you wondering?"

The old man gave Meadows a defiant look, lifting his chin. "I was wonderin' just how much of a kindness you'd deem it fer somebody to come along an' put you out of yore misery was you hurt. I don't reckon you'd think it such a boon."

Meadows stared at him. "You are an old man, Mr. Hatch. Don't think that your age is protection against my displeasure."

He turned to look back at Longarm. "How about you, Mr. Long? Do you consider my choice realistic or cruel?"

Longarm smiled thinly. "I never reckoned he should have been hit in the head with a rifle stock in the first place. I took one in the chest and I guess that kind of influences my opinion."

"So you did, Mr. Long. I had forgotten. You were riding to what you thought was the defense of a lady. I assume you have learned better since."

"Lady or not, she seems to be doing a fair amount of pining. A kind word from you wouldn't be amiss."

They had moved down a little closer to the train. Hatch had lagged behind, but Longarm had stayed at James Meadows's shoulder. His plan was already formed.

Below them the squad was taking the portly man to the caboose, half carrying him and half dragging him. The two women who'd been nursing him were trying to tag along, but they were rushed back into line with the other passengers by a trooper wielding his rifle like a prod.

Longarm could see that the firing squad was having trouble with the portly man. They kept trying to lean him up against the caboose, only to have him crumple and fall to the ground.

Meadows called down, "Corporal Cupper! Your men are looking foolish! Get some cord and bind the man to the handhold at the end of the caboose! This is an execution, not a circus!"

Cupper saluted. "Yessir!"

"Be quick about it! I have said I will shoot this man at six P.M. and I will shoot him at that time."

"Yessir!"

Longarm watched the corporal go into the caboose and return with some short lengths of rope. With the help of the other four men he got the wounded man next to a handhold and, by trussing him under the shoulders, was able to hang him in an upright position.

Longarm said, "What difference does it make if he's standing up or not, Lieutenant? Dead is dead, ain't it?"

Meadows turned his head and gave him a severe look. "There are traditions to be observed, Mr. Long. As a civilian I don't expect you would understand that." He transferred his attention down to the train. "Corporal Cupper! Form your firing squad! Make the distance seven paces!" He looked around at Longarm. "As a gambler I'm sure you will approve of the number."

"Seems like one bullet in the head would do the job just as good as all this pomp and ceremony."

"As I say, Mr. Long, there are certain protocols I don't expect you to understand." He stepped backwards.

The move put him only a couple of feet in front of Longarm and slightly to the lawman's right. Longarm had his right hand resting on his belt buckle, his fingers ready to reach in and pluck out the derringer. He kept hoping that he would not have to expose himself, but it was becoming all too clear that Meadows intended to go through with his gruesome charade. He could hear some of the women wailing, and moaning and grumbling from the men.

Below, the firing squad had formed. The four men were down on one knee, waiting for the order to mount arms. Corporal Cupper gave it. Their rifles came to their shoulders. Cupper said, "Aim!"

At that instant Longarm drew the derringer with his right hand and with his left arm clenched Meadows's neck in an armlock as he jammed the small gun into the small of Meadows's back. He had expected the man to try and jerk free, so he had slid his right leg in between Meadows's legs and pulled him back by the arm he had around the man's neck. But Meadows did not make a move other than to stiffen. Longarm said quietly, "*Lieutenant,* what you feel pressing right up against your spine is a Smith & Wesson .38-caliber derringer. Double-barreled. Over-and-under. I put both slugs into your spine you are going to walk mighty funny. You understand me?"

"I hear you, Mr. Long. What is your game?"

"It ain't a game, Meadows. You make the slightest move and you will find that out to your sorrow. Now, I want you to yell to that corporal and tell him to order that squad to put their guns down. Then I want them all to raise their hands and walk clean away from their rifles. You understand?"

"Yes. I hear you, Mr. Long. However, you are constricting my throat so that I can not yell."

Only then did Longarm become aware of just how tightly he had the man bound by his clenched arm. Meadows's voice had been coming thin and in gasps. Longarm said, "All right. I am going to release some pressure. But if you try and jerk away, I have the hammers of this derringer cocked and I will fire both barrels at once. You are not faster than a bullet, Lieutenant. Keep that in mind."

He slowly released the tense pressure of his arm against Meadows's throat, but he keep a firm grip on the epaulet on Meadows's right shoulder with his hand. For compensation

146

he jammed the powerful little gun even harder into the deserter's back.

Meadows gasped for a moment and then cleared his throat. He coughed and then took a breath.

Longarm whispered fiercely into his ear, "Get on with it!"

"Corporal!"

Corporal Cupper turned and looked toward Meadows. If he was surprised at what he saw he made no sign. "Sir!"

"Corporal, have your men come to their feet."

"Yes, sir!"

Longarm said, "Tell them to put them goddamn rifles down. Now!"

"Corporal, have your men immediately train their rifles on the crowd. If this man behind me fires a shot you are to immediately commence firing on the passengers! Do you understand!"

"Yes, sir!" To the four troopers Cupper said, "Squad right! Arms to bear!"

Longarm said, "Recall that order or I will blow you in two!" He was stunned by the move. It had caught him unexpectedly. If anything he had expected Meadows to order his men to fire on *him*. He had been ready for that and had been ready to pay the price. Since he had drawn the derringer he hadn't given himself much chance of getting out of the gamble alive. But this new development had him at a loss as to how to handle it. He had no doubt whatsoever that, if he fired, Cupper's men would begin to cutdown the passengers. He couldn't have that.

He said, "Meadows, it ain't gonna work. You and I are just going to stand here and see who has got the most nerve. I'm a very patient man. And it ain't me got a bulldog gun pressed up against his backbone. Ever see an old steer trying to drag himself around with a broken back? It's a awful sight, Meadows. And this is scaring me. My hand might go to shaking."

Meadows suddenly called out, "Corporal, count to ten. At ten you are to fire on the—"

He got no further because Longarm clamped off his wind with an iron forearm. He said, "No, you don't, you sonofabitch!"

But he was too late. Cupper had appraised the situation and he knew what his leader wanted. He said, in a loud, clear voice, "One . . . two . . . three . . ."

Longarm could see the line of passengers shrinking back from the rifles that were pointed at them. He could see Janice's fearful face looking his way.

" . . . four . . . five . . . six . . ."

A woman screamed. A couple of the men tried to crouch down as if to get under the train.

" . . . seven . . . eight . . ."

Longarm suddenly released his grip and lowered the derringer. "You win, Meadows. Tell your corporal to stop counting."

"Corporal Cupper!"

"Sir!"

"Stand easy. Order your men to ground their rifles."

"Yessir!"

"But keep your eye on Mr. Long here."

"Yessir! Squad, about face. Cover the lootenant!"

Meadows turned around to face Longarm. He took the derringer out of the deputy marshal's hand. Longarm said, "You won that hand, Meadows. I don't know if you were bluffing or not, but the stakes just got too high for me to call."

Meadows looked at the small pistol, then looked up into Longarm's eyes. "I told you, Mr. Long. I don't bluff. Do you have any other firearms secreted about your person?"

"No. I got a stiletto knife in my boot, but that's it."

"Take it out and throw it on the ground."

Longarm bent and did so. When he straightened up he said, "Why don't you let me take that man's place? You're going to shoot me anyway. One example is as good as another."

Meadows looked surprised. "I have no intentions of shooting you, Mr. Long, unless you force me to. I have admiration for brave men. What you did was an act of courage."

"Then for God's sake, don't let it be for nothing. Don't shoot that poor bastard. Mr. Hatch will lie and say you did. So will I if somebody will show me how to operate that telegraph."

"Stand in front of me, Mr. Long. Two steps forward, if you please."

Longarm took two slow steps forward. It moved him just past Meadows.

Meadows called down, "Corporal Cupper, we are now four minutes past our time. Form your squad and carry out your orders."

Longarm was looking at the ground when he heard the command "FIRE!" and heard the loud rattle of the four rifles. He looked up to see the portly man sag down against the ropes that held him to the caboose. The elk tooth swung freely back and forth at the end of its gold chain. Longarm could see the blood starting to seep through the man's tweed vest. It was all near the area of his heart. That, Longarm thought, was at least good. The soldiers had been excellent shots and the man had died instantly.

He said, "Shit!"

From behind him Meadows called down, "Corporal Cupper!"

"Sir!"

"Detail two men to bury the dead man. You and one other trooper are to come here immediately and search Mr. Long to make sure he is not carrying other concealed weapons."

"Yessir!"

Meadows turned and looked at Longarm. "I hope you will not resent this, Mr. Long. I cannot say it was a very pleasant sensation to have this gun pressed against my back."

Longarm shrugged. "I didn't much enjoy the sensation of seeing rifles pointed at innocent people and knowing you'd think no more of killing them than you'd think of gunning down a mad dog."

He could see Cupper and another trooper advancing on him. He knew what they were going to find in his left shirt pocket. He thought he'd save them the trouble.

Meadows said, "You realize you'll have to stand punishment. I can't let an act like this pass unobserved. It would be bad for morale. I have my duty."

"Yes," Longarm said, "and I had mine." He dug into his left pocket and took out his badge. "I am a deputy United States marshal and it was my duty to keep you from killing that man."

Meadows stared at the badge in Longarm's palm and then up into his eyes. He said, "By George, sir! You are an officer. A federal officer!"

Chapter 9

The idea of punishment seemed to go out of Meadows's head the minute he realized that Longarm was a federal officer. He still had Cupper and the other trooper search Longarm, but he said, "Can't blame a man for doing his duty. In fact it was a damn brave act, Marshal Long. Damn brave."

He said to Cupper and the other trooper, "This gentleman is to be treated with the respect due an officer. Is that clear?"

They both said in unison, "Yessir!"

Longarm stared at him in amazement. He was convinced the man was insane. If someone had just pulled the same trick on him, he'd have had them down on the ground licking dirt and begging for their lives.

Meadows said, "It's time we contacted your company, Conductor. You look a little pale around the gills. Never saw a man shot before?"

Hatch was stooped even lower than before. As they trooped up toward the telegraph table Longarm thought he saw tears in the old man's eyes. Hatch said, "Never lost a passenger. All them years. Never lost a one. Had a few babies born, but never had nobody die. Had one old gent come down with a sharp pain in his chest. Heard he died right soon, but he never done it on my train."

Longarm patted him softly on the back and said, "Hang on, Mr. Hatch. Some evening up of the score is about over-due."

Meadows said, "You are quite a prize for me, Marshal Long. We'll see what they have to say when they understand I've got a federal marshal in my custody. They might not be so quick to send troops if they realize they'll be killing one of their own."

Longarm smiled thinly. "Meadows, I don't reckon you know much about the marshal service. We're about as valu-able as old shoes. You kill me or get me killed, I'll just be one more off the payroll to my boss. We ain't very important as a class of peace officers."

Meadows laughed. "You play the game very well, Mar-shal Long." His face closed. "However, I know different. I've seen federal marshals come onto posts I've been sta-tioned at. They can walk up to the post commander and requisition anything they need from horses to troops to guns to toffee candy. Don't use that line on me. There ain't a hell of a lot of you and you are held in rather high esteem. In the field you can be judge, jury, and hangman. Tell it to somebody who hasn't seen one of your bunch."

Longarm just stared back.

Meadows turned to Cupper. "Go get the passengers set-tled. All I'll need here is Hanks." As Cupper started to turn away Meadows said, "Oh, here." He handed him the derringer. "Put that away somewhere. That's what he had in my back. Would have made a hell of a hole, don't you see." He glanced at Longarm. "Where did you have it hid?"

"In my boot," Longarm lied. He was still annoyed and angry at the way Meadows had gotten around him. Meadows seemed to sense it, because he stared at Longarm and asked Cupper how he thought the situation had been handled.

The corporal said, "First-rate, sir. I seen that you was in a little trouble, and was wonderin' what I ought to do when you give the exact right order. I reckon that's why you got the gold bars and I got the stripes."

"That's right, Corporal," Meadows said. He smiled at Longarm. "It's not every day I get a chance to outsmart a federal marshal. I've seen plenty of them swaggering around forts I was stationed at, but I never had the chance of having one in my power."

Longarm said, "You didn't outsmart me, Meadows. You just out-lowlifed me. I put the lives of those people above the pleasure of blowing you in half."

Meadows laughed. "Oh, be a good sport about it, Marshal Long. See the funny side. I can." He turned to Hatch, who was seated at the table. "Are you ready, Mr. Hatch? Step up here, Hanks, and get your ears on. We shall see what the railroads have to say now about their inability to protect their passengers. I don't think it is going to be very good for their business once word gets around. I believe you did say, Mr. Hatch, that this was an open wire and all sorts of interested parties might be listening in?"

Hatch didn't bother to even nod, just let his head hang lower.

Meadows said, "Now, Mr. Hatch, send the following statement. It is to be from Lieutenant James Meadows, commanding, incursion party, U.S. Army detached. Are you ready?"

Hatch nodded wearily.

"In accordance with my conditions and your failure to meet your obligations to your passengers, I have today caused to be executed one Joel Rayland of St. Louis.

153

His execution took place at six-oh-four this P.M. I now advise you you have until noon tomorrow to deliver me one hundred and fifty thousand dollars, half in cash and half in gold, or another execution will occur. Be assured I am ready to execute passengers until they are all finished. The deadlines between executions will continue to diminish so you should not expect to have the time to bring troops into position against me. Await your answer."

Hatch finished tapping a half a minute after Meadows's message. He sat back, waiting for the return message. He looked around at Meadows with dull eyes. "They'll be talking. Might take a few minutes."

Meadows said, "Huh! They had better realize that I am tired of their talking." He slammed one gloved fist into the palm of the other. "I want action, I want my money!"

Longarm just stared at him, wondering if the railroad realized they were dealing with an insane man.

The key started chattering. The message lasted less than a minute. It was Hanks who interpreted it for Meadows. "Lootenant, they ain't real happy. They claim they is tryin' their best to git up yore money and they begs you not to exa—exu—shoot anybody else till they can get this ball rollin'. They say they are makin' all kinds of efforts."

Meadows said to Hatch, "Send this message. Tell them I have in my custody a United States deputy marshal. His name is Long. Custis Long. Advise them that if they send troops Mr. Marshal Long will be standing out in front to stop the first bullet."

Hatch sent the wire and then sat back. In a very few moments a return message was coming in. Hatch wrote on a paper as he listened. When the key went silent he said, "They ask for Marshal Long's identification number and any other information he can send to further identify himself."

154

Longarm said, "My badge number is five-one-two. It is engraved on the back of my tin. I work out of Denver, Colorado, and my boss is Chief Marshal Billy Vail."

He stared at Meadows while he said it. Hatch looked around to Meadows. "Shall I send it?"

"Of course. I don't want them thinking I have a made-up marshal anymore than I want to believing I am not really going to shoot their passengers."

While Hatch was handling the message, Longarm walked off a few paces and stared at the wagons and the line of horses on the picket rope. He wondered how tightly they were tied, if they could be scared off with a few gunshots. He could go to the train, somehow secrete the six-shooter about his person, and have a try at running off the deserters' horses. But he'd have to make sure they were all scattered. If one was caught, he could be used to round the rest up.

Longarm turned back. It didn't seem like a very good idea.

Hatch said, looking at Longarm, "Mr. Long—I mean, Marshal Long, the company requests you do your best to reach some sort of compromise with Lieutenant Meadows in order to prevent further bloodshed. They have wired your boss, Marshal Vail, and are awaiting word from him. But meanwhile, since you are on the scene, they ask that you try and reach an understanding with Lieutenant Meadows."

Longarm fixed Meadows with his eyes. "Tell them that the only compromise I'll reach with this sonofabitch of a sidewinder is the immediate and unconditional surrender of him and his men. They lay down their arms now and I promise I won't roast their balls over a slow fire. That's the only deal I'm willing to make."

Meadows said quickly, "Don't send that." Then he turned slowly and looked at Longarm. "Marshal Long, I think you are forgetting yourself. I have treated you with the respect

155

due your rank. I would expect the same courtesy from you."

Longarm's eyes were hard slits. He knew he was on dangerous ground, but he could not help himself. He had played up to this criminal maniac as long as he could. He said, "You ain't got no rank, you sonofabitch! You are a deserter. You ain't no cavalry officer. And your men aren't troops. You are nothing but an outlaw gang that is fair game to any man with the law on his mind and a gun in his hand. You are a bank robber. You are a murderer. You are the lowest sonofabitch I believe I ever saw. Surrender to me right now and I'll do my best to keep the passengers from tearing you limb from limb."

Meadows's face had gotten whiter and whiter as Longarm spoke. His mouth had pinched together. Now he said, in a strangled voice, "Marshal Long, you will go to your place on the train and you will stay there! Do you hear me! We will see who is the officer here and who knows how to comport himself! Now begone from me!"

Longarm said, "You better think over my offer. I would reckon there are real army troops not twenty miles from here and advancing."

Meadows raised his arm and pointed. "Get to that train and get inside and stay there! Trooper Hanks, escort this man."

"Yessir."

Longarm turned his back and slowly started the two-hundred-yard walk to the train. He could see the passengers with their heads out the windows watching him. He was sure that many had wondered about his role, about his presence near Meadows on so many occasions.

Hanks said, "Here come the lootenant. Likely he has changed his mind an' iz gonna shoot yore ass now."

Longarm glanced back. Meadows was striding rapidly after them, and said, "Long, you are not to step off that

156

train for any reason! Do you understand me?"

Longarm glanced back, but kept walking. He heard Meadows yelling behind him "You there! You sentries on top of the train! Attention!"

Longarm glanced up to see the two men on guard on top of the train come to attention, their rifles grounded by their sides. Meadows was yelling again. "Do you see this man? Observe him closely. He is not to set foot outside of that train. If he does you are to shoot him. But you are to shoot him to wound. Do not kill him! Do you understand?"

Longarm was close to the train now and he heard the two sentries say, "Yessir!" in unison.

"Long!"

Longarm was at the door of the coach, about to mount the first step. He looked back. Meadows said, "It will be you who will be executed at noon tomorrow! Do you understand me, Long! I'll have you shot tomorrow! Then we will see who is the officer here and who is in command."

Longarm just gave him a shrug, and stepped into the relative cool of the vestibule. He glanced back out. Meadows was still staring after him, his anger still hot. Longarm thought, I was told he didn't get angry. Looks angry to me.

"Shot, Long! Shot like that drummer from St. Louis!"

Longarm just shook his head and opened the door to his coach. As he stepped in he immediately saw Janice. She was sitting with Carol Ann. She turned a tear-stained face to him and said, "Oh, Mr. Long! I was so worried about you. I was afraid they'd kill you."

She jumped up and embraced him in the aisle. Over her shoulder Longarm could see Carol Ann sitting back in the corner, staring stonily ahead. Up front the few passengers still in his car looked back his way, puzzlement clear on

157

their faces. Once he had shown his badge to Meadows he'd had no further need to conceal it. Now he wore it pinned to the flap of his shirt pocket.

With gentle hands he disengaged her arms from around his neck, saying, "Honey, I don't reckon you better sit with me for the time being. Right now I ain't in real good with the boys that has got the guns. You set right back down by Carol Ann and comfort her."

He guided her back into her seat and then sat down across the aisle from her, adding, "It's all got a little bit more complicated, and I ain't sure that Mr. Meadows ain't about to slip his halter."

She wiped at her eyes. "But what's it all about? Did you see them shoot that man? I could not believe that James would actually go so far. He can be so cruel. Oh! You've got your badge on. Does that mean he knows?"

As briefly as he could Longarm explained what had happened, not leaving out how he had been outsmarted when Meadows had had the rifles turned on the crowd.

Janice stared at him, her mouth open. "And so that was why they swung the rifles at us. Lordy, I thought I was going to faint. I thought we were all going to be seeing the archangel at any second. And you had a gun in his back? Where did you get a gun?"

Longarm showed her his big concave buckle and how it had been fitted out to conceal the derringer.

She said, "Why, that is ever so clever."

Longarm shrugged. "Not as clever as Meadows. He gambled your lives and won."

"What do you think is going to happen now."

Before he could answer the rear door of the coach opened and Meadows suddenly appeared. He stopped just inside and shouted down the length of the car. "Be advised, Marshal Long, that we have notified the railroad company just who it is who is going to be shot tomorrow at noon if I don't have my money."

Longarm said, "If you plan to shoot me I reckon you had better bring your lunch."

"What do you mean by that nonsense remark?"

"I mean you might find it's an all-day job. That's what I mean by that nonsense remark. You might get hungry."

Meadows stared at him for a full half second, then turned on his heel. As he exited the car he said, "We will see, Marshal Long. We will see."

Janice turned stricken eyes to him. "He doesn't mean it! Surely! He promised us there would be no killing. I never thought he would shoot that poor man with the hurt head. And now he is talking of you! I won't hear of it!" She started out of her seat, but Longarm reached out and restrained her. "Janice, honey, the time to fool around with a bear ain't when he's got a mad on. Let it rest. It ain't a real good idea to go around shooting U.S. deputy marshals and Meadows knows it."

She sat back, staring at the door through which Meadows had vanished. "I hate him," she said with force. "I hate him! I hate him! First he hurt Carol Ann and now he is proposing to shoot you!"

Outside it was coming dusk. Up near the little patch of mesquite trees Longarm could see a fire beginning to flare up. He reckoned it was the cookfire that whoever did the vittles for the deserters was getting started for supper. It reminded him of just how hungry he was himself. He yawned and sat back in his seat. He'd made a supper out of air before and he reckoned he could do it again. The coach was growing dimmer. In a natural movement, as if stretching out, he slid his upper body across the seat until he was leaning against the coach wall. A few of the passengers were moving around, some of them going to the little toilet that was at the front of the car, some coming his way to see how much water was left in the big keg just outside the door in the vestibule. Besides himself and Janice and Carol Ann, there were now three men and two women in the coach. A few had moved out to get away from the moaning of Rayland. Well, Longarm thought, he was out of his pain now.

When the aisle was clear Longarm carefully felt down in the space between his seat and the wall. His fingers touched the reassuring butt of his revolver. He reckoned Meadows was in for a surprise when he came to take him out to shoot him. The lieutenant might find himself with a chore on his hands trying to raise a squad of four men to do the shooting. Longarm had six cartridges and he did not intend to miss with any of them. He thought of trying to get the little .25-caliber back from Carol Ann, but deemed it more trouble than it was worth. Shoot an armed man with a weapon like that and, if you didn't hit him in the eye or some similar place, you'd just make him mad as hell and give him more determination to finish you off.

He stared out the window at the growing dark. The moon would be up soon, he reckoned. He did not wonder if it might be the last moon he'd ever see because he didn't think that way. He'd been in many tight spots in his career as a federal officer and he had never doubted that he'd find a way out. He had to admit to himself, just at that moment, that none were occurring to him, but he had faith he'd think of something. He smiled, thinking of Billy Vail, who always claimed that Longarm needlessly complicated situations just so he could look smart when he worked his way clear. Billy had said, "If you'd spend more time figuring out how to *stay* out of trouble, you wouldn't have to spend so damn much effort *getting* out of it."

There was a very little whiskey left in his only bottle.

160

When the troopers had searched his saddlebags they'd confiscated his second bottle. All the whiskey-laced cider, of course, was gone. He had only a little less than a quarter of a bottle left to last the night. Well, he thought, it didn't matter. He was tired and would most likely sleep the dark hours away. He reckoned it would be handy if he were well rested the next day as he expected matters to get a little lively. There was, of course, a chance that real troopers might arrive before noon the next day, but he doubted it. If they came by train they still had a good five miles to advance overland, and Meadows would be able to keep them pinned down for a considerable time.

He'd also have time to send a man to dispatch Deputy U.S. Marshal Custis Long.

He had a small drink and then lit a cigar and leaned back against the wall. His fingers felt down in the crack again and touched the flare gun. It was a weapon but he was damned if he knew how to use it or what for. It wasn't very accurate and it didn't have much range, but it was better than throwing a cud of tobacco at someone.

He looked across and studied Janice in profile. She was sure as hell one pretty woman, and the thought of her body made his jeans want to bulge out. He wondered what Meadows had planned for the two of them, Janice and Carol Ann. At just that instant she turned to look at him, and they both smiled. It was getting too dark to see, but her teeth were white in the gloom and her blond hair seemed to have a glow about it. The peroxide, he reckoned. He didn't think he'd ever figure out why a woman with a head of red hair would want to tone it down, as beautiful as her pubic hair was.

He yawned, stubbed out his cigar, and decided he'd take a nap for a couple of hours. If Meadows was going to try to slip on the train and do him harm, he'd come late. But Longarm doubted he'd do such a thing. Meadows wanted to play soldier and execute him in front of a crowd. That was his style.

After a while Longarm slept. Sometime during the night he was aware that Janice had slipped into the seat with him. He cuddled her in his arms and felt her head on his chest. Her hair was just under his chin and he thought it smelled mighty fresh for something that had been dyed.

Once he woke and, being careful not to wake Janice, lit a cigar and took another small drink of whiskey. He spent an hour smoking and listening and looking, and then put his cigar out and went back to sleep.

It was light when he awoke. It startled him to instant wakefulness, the sun streaming into the coach and people up moving around. Many a night had passed since he'd let the sun catch him with his eyes closed. He fumbled out his watch and took a quick look. It was a few minutes before seven. At least it had not been light for very long. He sat up and looked around. Janice was gone, but Carol Ann was sitting as she had been the night before, bolt upright in her seat, her hands in her lap clutching her handbag, staring straight ahead. He said, "Good morning, Carol Ann," but she made no sign she'd heard.

He stood up, went out into the vestibule, and got a dipper of water and drank it. The top of the outside door was open, and he glanced out to see the deserters' camp slowly coming to life. Here and there a trooper walked with his suspenders down, or was standing and knotting his yellow kerchief around his neck. They hadn't been up long either, Longarm calculated. There was no sign of Janice. He figured she was stretching her legs or in the toilet.

He went back to his seat and treated himself to a small sip of whiskey by way of breakfast. After a little searching he found the stub of the cigar he'd been smoking the night

162

before and got it lit and drawing. He had one cigar left besides the stub. He said, "Carol Ann, matters are getting desperate. I'm down to one cigar and damn little whiskey. What do you think of that?"

She didn't move or reply.

He said, "Carol Ann, you got to come out of this. You are going to turn to stone pretty soon."

When she still wouldn't respond he gave it up for a bad job, and looked out the window in time to see one trooper coming down the steel ladder on the side of the car and another going up. He said to the one mounting the rungs, "Call down if you see the real cavalry coming."

The trooper was a hard-faced young man Longarm didn't know the name of. He gave Longarm a glare and kept climbing, his rifle slung over his shoulder.

Longarm settled himself down to wait. By his watch it was half past seven. If Meadows intended to carry out his threat, Longarm figured he'd be coming along in about four hours. If he did he'd never see noon or any other time once he announced his intentions.

Longarm was starting to worry about Janice when she suddenly came back into the coach. She gave him a quick smile, but instead of joining him, she got into the seat across from Carol Ann. Once there she did a strange thing. She leaned across and whispered something in Carol Ann's ear that Longarm couldn't hear, and Carol Ann immediately shifted her position to the aisle seat. Then Janice crossed the space between the seats and sat down beside Carol Ann, where she had been sitting. As Longarm watched in puzzlement Janice leaned her head close to Carol Ann's ear and seemed to be talking to her in a low, urgent voice. Longarm could only hear a faint murmur, but occasionally, Carol Ann would nod her head emphatically. Longarm hated to shift his position to the aisle seat. It would be too obvious. But he was mighty curious about what was going on and what was being said. If the two women were up to something, he thought they had better let him in on their plans since, so far as he knew, he was the only armed man among the passengers.

But hell, he thought, maybe Janice was trying to talk Carol Ann into making some kind of appeal to Meadows. It wouldn't work, but anything was worth a try.

He was slowly edging his way toward the aisle so that he could try to overhear what was being said, when the rear door of the coach was suddenly slammed back and James Meadows stood there. Behind him Longarm could see what appeared to be two more troopers. He had expected Meadows's eyes to come straight to him, but instead he seemed to be staring at the corner where the two women, Janice and Carol Ann, were.

He paused for just a half a second, and then he came through the door followed by the troopers, both with rifles at port arms. There was no doubt now that he was heading for the women. His eyes were fixed directly on one or the other or both of them, and as he got into the aisle, his right hand came up and began fumbling with the cover of his military holster. He had his pistol half drawn when Longarm suddenly became aware of Carol Ann standing in the aisle next to him. She had her arm out straight and pointed down the aisle at Meadows. In her hand he saw the glint of the little silver-plated pistol. Longarm heard Meadows say, "Carol Ann! Put that—"

Then there was a sudden *pop, pop, pop,* and Longarm saw a little pink spot suddenly appear on the blue sleeve of Meadows's upper right arm. There was another *pop* and another pink spot suddenly showed on Meadows's left side. Longarm saw him stagger a step backwards, heard the clatter as Meadows dropped his pistol on the floor. He saw

Meadows melting back into the two troopers as they shouldered their way forward, their rifles raised in a firing position. Longarm was starting to whirl to his left to dig out his Colt with the nine-inch barrel when he heard a loud explosion and, out of the corner of his eye, saw Carol Ann flung suddenly backwards as if struck by a giant hand.

He had not been aware that he had been yelling until he heard his own words following the echo of the shot that had killed Carol Ann. His echo was yelling, "Down, down! Get down, Janice!"

Then he saw both rifles searching around, looking for another target. He hunched low as he came out of the little crevice with his Colt .44. He had the hammer thumbed back as he brought the barrel over the edge of the seat in front of him. He shot the first trooper dead in the chest, hitting him so solidly that the man flipped his rifle in the air and fell straight backwards. But there was no time to pause. He vaguely realized it was Corporal Cupper who was trying to bring his rifle to bear as the trooper who'd just been shot fell back into him. Longarm had his revolver recocked, and was already making the shot on Cupper while part of his eye tracked the stumbling progress of Meadows as he tried to get out of the car.

His shot hit Cupper a little high, taking him in the collarbone just below the throat. The slug hit enough bone to knock Cupper down, and tore through the throat sufficiently so that a great gout of blood spewed forth as Cupper went down.

Longarm barely saw it. Once he saw Cupper start backwards, he swung his gun to the left, trying to catch Meadows before he could get out of the car. He was still struggling with the door as Longarm thumbed back the hammer for an easy shot. At that instant one of the plump ladies who'd tried to nurse Rayland suddenly sat up in her seat, blocking his

165

shot. He screamed, "Down! Down, goddammit!" and slid to his left. Meadows was nearly through the door before he could fire. The gun slammed back in his palm, but all he saw was some chips fly from the door as Meadows let it close behind him.

He stood up, swearing. He took time to glance at Janice. She was huddled on the floor. Her upturned face was pale and frightened, but she didn't appear to be hurt. He jumped into the aisle and started toward the rear of the car. He paused to scoop up the revolver that Meadows had dropped, fully aware that he had only three cartridges left in his own gun and that there were five armed deserters against him. Maybe six, if Meadows wasn't hurt too bad.

He jumped over the first trooper, and then had to shove one of the women aside as she was hysterically trying to climb out into the aisle. He took a step, and almost slipped and fell in the blood that was still flowing from Corporal Cupper's throat. He got around the body, jerked at the door handle, and rushed into the vestibule. The door to the west side was closed top and bottom. He held both revolvers in his left hand and jerked the door open with his right.

He was halfway down the steps, looking left and right and straight ahead for Meadows, when a bullet suddenly zinged right by his ear and buried itself in the ground at the bottom of the steps. He instantly jumped back, realizing it was the sentry on the roof. He transferred his revolver to his right hand and fired into the ceiling of the vestibule, not knowing if a bullet would penetrate it or not.

Almost instantly he heard a bang above him and a bullet came tearing through the ceiling, struck the metal floor, and ricocheted off and into the other door. Without pause Longarm pointed Meadows's .45-caliber revolver at the hole the rifle bullet had made coming through the ceiling and fired three quick shots. For a second he thought nothing had happened, but then he heard a strangled cry, and turned just in time to see the trooper come falling by the open door and hit the ground with a thump. He lay still. Longarm could see blood staining the blue of his uniform pants at the crotch. "Damn!" he said aloud. Hell of a place to get hit, he thought.

But he knew he had no time to think about anything. He had to get the passengers bunched so he could protect them, and he had to keep Meadows from organizing his remaining troops. He pushed through the door and started down the aisle. He yelled, "Stay in your seats! Stay below the windows! Get on the floor! Hurry, hurry! HURRY GODDAMMIT!"

He stopped to stick Meadows's revolver in his belt, and then stooped to catch up the two Springfield rifles by their slings where they lay by the bodies on the floor. A woman was screaming but he took no notice. He ran, stooped, up to the front of the car, and ducked down by where Janice was crouched. She looked up at him, her eyes terrified. "Oh, Mr. Long, what is going to happen now?"

He said harshly, "We're all going to get killed if you don't do what I tell you right now. I want you to go back to the next car and get the rest of the passengers up here in this one. I can't protect all of them if they're scattered. If Meadows gets his hands on some more hostages I'm finished. You've got to go and you've got to go now."

On hands and knees she peeked around her seat down the aisle. She said, her voice quavering, "I can't. They are dead."

He reached out and slapped her lightly. "Janice, I don't have time to mess with you. I've got to get the rest of my equipment and set up a firing station. Now move or don't. I ain't got the time."

He turned away and crawled over his seat to where he

had the flare gun and the cartridges cached. In a moment he had them in hand. Behind him he heard Janice say, "But I thought she would kill him."

He gave what she said no thought, just noted, with satisfaction, that she was making her way down the aisle, walking stooped over. With his arms full of rifles and guns and his pockets full of flare cartridges, he started toward the door that led into the vestibule. Carol Ann was lying against the back wall, her long skirt up over her knees, her chest covered with blood. Her eyes were wide open, staring vacantly. He felt a beat of pity, but he had no time for the dead. There were still too many very much alive with guns and hostile intentions who had to be dealt with first. With an awkward effort he pulled open the door into the vestibule, and managed to work his way through carrying his load. He made sure the eastward-facing half door was shut so that he couldn't be taken from behind, and then dropped his load of weapons in front of the other door that had the top half open. He crouched against it for a second, and then slowly raised his head to just lift an eye over the top.

Chapter 10

At first there was nothing to see. The "parade ground" was deserted except for the telegrapher's table sitting up on the little rise a hundred or so yards away. Hatch was nowhere in sight. Longarm hoped that he had made it to some sort of safety and was not being held hostage by Meadows. But he had decided, once the fight began, that nothing would deter him. He was tired of having his hands tied by Meadows's methods. From here on in it was kill the enemy or allow them to surrender just as fast as possible.

Looking toward the wagons and the picket line of horses, he thought he saw a flash of blue here and there. He wondered where Meadows was, wondered if he was prowling along the side of the train waiting for an easy shot at him. But he couldn't think of that now. Right now he had to get the pot boiling, get the fight started.

He broke the flare gun and inserted one of the big cartridges. Then he eased up to the open half of the door and rested the barrel of the flare gun on it, trying to guess the angle required to drop one of the phosphorus flares into the wagons. He settled on an angle and pulled the trigger. It was like shooting off a July Fourth rocket. It didn't make a bang or give a recoil. Just all of a sudden a stream of smoke and sparks flew out the barrel of the gun.

He watched the ball of white fire, trailing smoke, arc across the light blue sky. Even before it landed he could tell he'd fired too high. The flare cleared the wagons by a good ten feet and splintered into a thousand sparks as it crashed into the stunted little mesquite beyond the wagons. As soon as he saw it land he ducked down below the level of the door. In an instant there came the rattle of half a dozen rifle shots. Some of them hit the lower door, but a few came through the top and ricocheted around inside the vestibule. One of them came a little too close for Longarm's comfort. A ricochet would kill you just as dead as a direct hit.

Holding the flare gun and dragging one of the rifles, he pushed open the door back into the coach and made his way inside. Then he got into a crouch and jumped into his seat, staying below the level of the window. He looked around, glad to see that Janice had succeeded in getting all the passengers gathered into the one car. He looked her way and saw that she was sitting in her seat, but was staying below the level of the window.

He said, "You all right?"

She gave him a quick little head bob and a weak smile. "I guess so. I got the people. They're all scared."

Longarm was inching his way toward his open window, breaking open the flare pistol and inserting another cartridge in it as he went. He said, "They got a right to be. Stay down. I think I am fixing to attract some attention."

He took his hat off and laid it on the seat, and then raised a cautious eye above the window ledge. Except for a little smoke rising over the clump of mesquite, not much had changed. He put the barrel of the pistol on the ledge of the window, adjusted the angle, and fired. He was able to watch just long enough to see the flare fall agonizingly short of the first wagon. He ducked down as the rattle of bullets hit the side of the coach and broke out his window and the one next to it.

Even before the firing had stopped he'd already moved three seats toward the rear of the coach, reloading the flare gun as he moved. He noted that none of the people had to be told to get down. They were all on the floor, even the fireman and the engineer.

He was quicker with his shot now because he felt instinctively that he had the range. He fired and watched the flare arc out and then drop, satisfyingly, onto the canvas cover of the second wagon. He ducked down as he saw it hit, waited for the gunfire to stop, and then came up quickly with one of the Springfield rifles. The canvas was already starting to burn and he saw a blue-clad figure burst from the mesquite and start for the wagon to put the fire out before it could get started good. Longarm had to make a snap shot, firing as he brought the rifle up. He saw the deserter skid to a stop and start back for the mesquite. Longarm rapidly worked the bolt to throw another cartridge into the chamber, and fired just as the man disappeared into the grove. He quickly fired two more shots into the area of the thicket where he'd seen the flashes of blue and then, working feverishly, reloaded the flare gun and fired another ball of phosphorus at the first wagon. Just before he ducked down behind the ledge he saw the the the canvas on the second wagon was well ignited and beginning to burn. After the expected burst of rifle fire he cautiously raised an eye over the window level. His shot at the first wagon had been an unusual hit. It had either hit the spoked wheel or the side of the wagon, because Longarm could see the body of the wagon catching fire as the old, dry wood was ignited by the fierce heat of the phosphorus.

He grabbed the rifle and flare gun and dashed back out into the vestibule, where he had left his pistol and the other rifle. He calculated that he had about seven rounds left in the Springfields, two shots left in his revolver, and three in the Navy Colt of Meadows. He could go for the rifle of the guard he'd shot off the roof. That would have two or three rounds left in it, and there might be more on the trooper's body, but he would be putting himself in the open and inviting a clear shot from a high-powered, accurate rifle.

He was in a tight fix and no mistake. He could not afford to trade shots with the deserters, but neither could he just sit and wait for them to attack. They'd come at night and they would come from several directions and he couldn't be everywhere at once.

He got an eye over the edge of the door, and was gratified to see that both wagons were beginning to burn fiercely. Now if the flames would only reach the powder he had broken out of the torpedoes, they might aid in igniting the blasting powder and the ammunition. If that happened he doubted the men that were hiding there could stay in the thicket of mesquite. The fire and the explosions would be too close.

He reloaded the flare gun and made a quick, arching shot aimed at the middle of the mesquite thicket. He didn't know if the gnarled old trees were close enough together to burn, but he thought it was worth a try. This time there came no barrage of shots, and it occurred to Longarm that his adversaries might be getting low on ammunition. Likely they had not carried a great amount on their persons since a fresh supply was in the wagons. But now that supply was cut off. He saw what he thought was a sign of a fire in the mesquite thicket. He loaded the flare gun with his last cartridge and sent it after the shot he had just fired. Then he picked up a Springfield and checked the magazine. It had three rounds left, and one in the chamber made four. Counting Meadows, there were five of the deserters left.

He'd killed three, and Carol Ann had wounded Meadows—how bad he had no way of knowing.

He wondered where Meadows was. It was difficult for him to believe that the man had managed to reach the mesquite and join up with his troops. Longarm had been right behind him, and he would have seen him if the man had gone running across the parade ground.

Of course Meadows could have ducked under the train and worked his way around to the right or the left to reach his base, and he could have easily done it without Longarm being able to spot him. So Longarm had to figure that the commander had rejoined his troops. That meant there would be some sort of coordinated attack. That was unless he could do something with the little ammunition he had left to stop it or break it up.

Just then he heard the first small explosion. He looked over the edge of the door and saw sparks flying in the air from the first wagon.

Once it began it only grew in volume and intensity. Explosion followed explosion until the wagons were torn apart and then the cases of cartridges began to pop. As the heat grew so did their intensity, until the wagons began to sound like Gatling guns. The horses and mules at the picket lines had grown crazed with fear and were jerking and pulling and bucking against their restraint. Longarm saw one horse wounded, and then saw a mule go down. The wagons were just smoldering heaps of white-hot fire that continually hissed out lethal pieces of lead. A trooper suddenly came charging out of the mesquite and made a run for a loose horse, grabbing at his hackamore, trying to mount. Longarm was just trying to get a steady shot at him when the trooper suddenly screamed and stumbled backwards, clawing at his back where he'd been hit by one of the flying bullets.

Now the whole thicket was beginning to burn. Longarm got up on one knee and rested the Springfield on the door ledge. Two troopers suddenly came racing out, one with a smoldering shirt. Longarm shot him first, seeing the bullet knock him sideways and send him into a roll. The other man was zigging and zagging. Unfortunately for him, he was doing it in a pattern. Longarm let the man zag away from him as he ran toward the north, and then shot him as he zigged back.

None of the three men had been Meadows. He wondered if Meadows was still in the burning thicket, wounded. He also wondered if there was still a sentry on top of the train. But he doubted that. Meadows had generally kept one sentry on top during the day and two at night. Still, one man was missing.

And then, in the distance, he saw a figure running due west. It was difficult because of the smoke to make out who the man might be. He doubted it was Meadows because the man was running at a good gait and Longarm doubted the deserter could have struck such a speed with two bullet holes in him, even two small bullet holes. Longarm lifted his rifle and considered taking a shot, but he didn't think it was necessary. The man wasn't carrying a gun, and more importantly, he didn't appear to be carrying any supplies or a canteen. It would be a waste of a bullet because the man would either have to come back or die in the desert.

That left only Meadows unaccounted for.

He waited. After fifteen minutes he went back into the coach and finished his whiskey and lit a cigar. He said loudly, "The fight ain't over. The one who claimed to be a lieutenant ain't been accounted for yet. I'm going to look for him. Stay in your seats. The sonofabitch is still dangerous."

174

He looked at Janice. "Are you all right?"

She looked calmer. "Yes. I'm fine. How are matters progressing?"

He said, "It's nearly over. I think. I got an idea where Meadows is. I'm going to look for him."

She put her hand to her throat. "Please be careful."

He smiled around his cigar. "How do you think I got so old?"

He went back through the door and into the vestibule. He had three cartridges in the Navy Colt and only two in his own revolver, but he stuck the .45 in his waistband and took his own revolver in his right hand. Then he opened the door and stepped down on the ground.

It seemed very quiet now after the tumult when the explosions were at their height. With regret he saw several horses down and one or two limping. The rest were running in circles, still frightened. He would have to tend to the wounded horses, but first there was Meadows to consider.

He had stayed very close to the car after he'd stepped down. The iron ladder to the roof was right beside him, and he turned and began a slow ascent, his revolver ready in his right hand, his eyes on any sign of movement over the edge of the roof. When he reached a point where he could raise his head and see atop the train he held his hat in his left hand and raised it up enough to draw fire if any was coming. Nothing happened, and he cautiously lifted his head and looked down the length of the train, to the left and to the right.

It was empty. Vacant.

He climbed the rest of the way and then stood, looking around in all directions. A tiny dot to the west identified the deserter who had chosen the desert to fire or surrender. He was still plodding along. Longarm figured he might last a few days, but no longer. If he hadn't had other business he would have chased the man down.

The wagons were still smoldering, but they had almost run their course. There was still a brisk blaze in the mesquite thicket, but Longarm knew it would die out as soon as the fire reached green wood.

Walking close to the center of the car so as not to present any better target than necessary, Longarm started toward the coal tender and the engine. Meadows, he figured, had to be either in one of those places or the caboose. He came quickly to the end of the coal tender and crouched down. The coal was in two long bins with a narrow walkway between them so the conductor could go from the coaches to the locomotive in order to consult with the engineer. The corridor was empty. Longarm looked the coal over carefully. He thought it would be very difficult for a man to burrow into the heaps to hide himself without leaving some strong sign of his presence. The coal looked undisturbed except for what might have been done by a shovel.

That left the cab.

Longarm jumped down, traversed the little passage in the coal tender, and then suddenly jumped into the cab. It was empty. He even opened the firebox with the idea that Meadows might have been so desperate as to cram himself in there and hope to get away at night. But one glance showed that not only was it empty, but that it would be too small to hold a grown man.

That left the caboose.

But first he walked around the engine to be sure that Meadows wasn't hiding on the cowcatcher. When it was clear the man was not at the front of the train he started toward the back, toward the caboose. The one thing that worried him was that Meadows might be in there with Hatch as hostage. If that was the case, he'd have a choice of keeping Meadows locked up until help arrived or letting him go in order to save Hatch's life.

He came to the end of the caboose, mounted the two steps, and tried the door. The handle turned, but the door would not open. It was held by the bolt that Longarm himself had thrown when he and Janice had sought privacy.

He banged on the door with the butt of his revolver. "Meadows! Meadows! Come on out of there or I will start shooting through this door! I've got a Springfield rifle here that will go through this door and you too. Now open up."

The door suddenly swung back, only it was Hatch standing there and not Meadows. Surprised, Longarm stepped back. "Is he in there?"

Hatch said, "No, praise the Lord. I barely beat him to the place. He was trying to get in when I slammed the door in his face and bolted the lock."

Longarm stepped down to the ground. Hatch followed him. The old man was looking even older and more tired, but he at least had his conductor's cap on. Longarm said, "He ain't outside. Not unless he's disguised as a cactus. And he ain't in the coaches or the engine or the tender. Where in hell can he be?"

Before he answered Hatch walked out a little way and looked around. He stared at the burned wagons and the mesquite thicket for a long moment. He turned to Longarm. "When all them loud noises commenced I never knowed what to think. Is it over then?"

Longarm fingered his gun. "It is except for Meadows. I expect he has somehow fled off across the badlands. Though I would have given him credit for more sense than that. The caboose is the last place I figured."

"Have you looked at the rods?"

Longarm gave him a blank look. "Rods?"

"Yessir. They are long connecting rods that run from axle to axle to support the undercarriage of the train. They are kind of flexible. A railroad undercarriage has got to have a little give to it."

"Where are they?"

"Well, they are under the cars. They run in pairs. Hoboes and tramps sometimes get in under the cars and lay on them. It is a mighty dangerous way to hitch a ride."

"What do I do?"

Hatch made a motion with his hand. "You got to lean down and look up under the car. You can't see them or anybody on them standing up."

"You wait here."

He walked around to the side of the caboose and looked. He saw the long rods, running in pairs, each about two inches in diameter, but he didn't see Meadows.

He walked to the middle of the second car and bent down. Even before he had stooped all the way over he saw the tail of a yellow kerchief hanging down. He straightened up and said, "Meadows, these are the last words I'm going to speak to you. You have thirty seconds to get out from under that car and surrender yourself or I am going to tell the passengers where you are and let them pull you out. I know you are not armed and I know how badly they would like to get their hands on you. The thirty seconds starts now."

Very few seconds had passed before a greasy and begrimed James Meadows came scrambling out from under the train. The minute he was erect he opened his mouth and started to babble. With a swift move Longarm whipped him across the face with the barrel of his pistol. He had the satisfaction of seeing blood spurt from Meadows's nose. Longarm said, "I forgot. I got one last thing to tell you. You open your mouth again and I'll beat you to death!"

Then he grabbed Meadows by the arm and began rapidly dragging him toward the caboose. Meadows stumbled along beside him, moaning and crying and trying to get a hand up to his face. Longarm never glanced at him, just dragged him along.

The ropes they'd used to bind Rayland to the caboose were still hanging from the iron handhold where they'd tied him. The red of his blood was in dark contrast to the rusty red of the peeling paint of the caboose.

Using both arms Longarm wheeled Meadows around and slammed him back-first against the caboose. With a few swift moves he lashed him as securely and tightly in place as he could. Then he stepped back and looked at the man he'd hated as hard as he'd reckoned he'd ever hated anyone. He had looked at him for not quite a minute when an unstoppable impulse came over him and he drew back his right fist and drove it into Meadow's side. The deserter made a moaning, whooshing sound and bent over as far as the ropes would let him. Without pause Longarm hit him with a fist in the left side, and had the satisfaction of feeling a bone crunch. He hit him with his right again, and was drawing his left back when the quiet voice of Hatch said from behind him, "I know how you feel, Marshal Long. But you are hurting yourself more than you are him."

With an effort Longarm stayed his fist. For just a second he stared into the eyes of Meadows, letting him know what he would really like to do. Finally he turned. He said wearily, "Mr. Hatch, would you please go up and telegraph and tell them that it is all over down here and would they please hurry because we got an awful lot of hungry and thirsty folks here. And besides that, I'm out of cigars and whiskey."

It took almost another twelve hours, but the railroad finally got the track fixed and reached them with a train out of

Odessa loaded with a detachment of cavalry troops and a few deputy sheriffs. Longarm turned Meadows over to the commander of the cavalry unit, and told him about the deserter who had taken off heading west. Longarm said, "You can chase him if you are of a mind, but I think the badlands will do your work for you."

Soon Longarm and Janice were on that same train as it rolled along at thirty miles an hour, backing all the way to Odessa. They were sitting facing the caboose so they wouldn't be riding backwards. Longarm had been able to find a few cigars and a bottle of whiskey from among their rescuers, and he and Janice were having a drink while he smoked a cigar. He said, "You know, Janice, all we been through, I still don't know your last name."

She said, "It's Meadows. Same as James."

He looked around at her. "The hell you say."

"We're half blood kin, though we don't put it about. Carol Ann never even knew. She thought we were cousins and she thought that was why James never wanted to make love to me, but that wouldn't have stopped the bastard."

Longarm said, "I am flummoxed. He knew you and I were going to use the caboose and what for. Hell, he called you common."

She tossed her head. "Oh, we never cared for one another at all. He thought I was common, and I thought he was so full of himself he ought to have floated off. I never saw a man put on such airs. But Carol Ann just loved it. The dumb bitch."

At first Longarm thought he'd heard wrong. He looked at her. "What did you say?"

"I said Carol Ann was a bitch. She was a dumb bitch. Did anything James wanted. I didn't mind when I saw it might lead to something, me getting the house."

"I thought you said you weren't proud of that."

"I'm not, not really." But then she turned an eager face to him. "But I'll tell you what I am proud of and I did it for you. And you probably thought it just happened."

He frowned. "What?"

She said proudly, "I made James come after Carol Ann and I convinced Carol Ann he was coming to kill her. She'd reached the state of mind where she would use that little pistol. I saw it in her. I knew her awfully well, you know."

Longarm was staggered. "Let me get this straight. Are you telling me it was your work that brought Meadows aboard that car with that look in his eye and drawing that pistol?"

"Oh, yes. You remember I wasn't there when you woke up yesterday morning?"

"Yeeess," Longarm said, staring at her.

"Well, I had gone to talk to James. We don't like each other, but he thinks I'm smart and he believes everything I tell him. I told him that Carol Ann was telling the rest of the passengers that he was wrecking the train to keep from marrying her because he couldn't make love to women. And I told him that she had a gun in her purse and she was going to shoot him in the face to mess up his good looks at the first chance she got. Of course I'd been working on Carol Ann the night before. When I come back I guess you saw me sit down by her and talk real quiet to her?"

Longarm felt himself going cold inside. He just nodded.

She said, "I told Carol Ann her only chance was to get up the next time James got on the train and shoot him, that she'd never have him or any self-respect if she didn't. And then I told her he planned to kill her. So of course when he came on there reaching for his pistol, the rest was just natural." She smiled. "Aren't you pleased with me? I done it all for you."

181

Longarm let out a breath and stood up. He stared at the far end of the car.

She said, "Where are you going?"

He reached down and picked up his bottle of whiskey. "I'm going to sit somewhere else. You can consider yourself under arrest."

"What? Under arrest?" The smile was fading from her face. "For what?"

"For accessory to murder. For inciting to riot. For interfering with a federal officer in the discharge of his duty. I'll probably think of a few more charges by the time we get to Odessa. I'm going to turn you over to the authorities there. I don't want to ride no further with you than I have to."

She started to rise. "Now just a damn minute!"

He put the palm of his hand on her perfect breast and shoved her back in the seat. He pointed a finger at her. "Don't get out of that chair again without I say you can."

Her face flamed red. "Now listen here, you! I—"

"No, *you* listen. Carol Ann was supposed to be your friend and you got her killed just so you could run her whorehouse. You ain't a hell of a lot different than James. You sure you ain't full blood kin? I know one thing. I'm sorry I ever laid with you. First chance I get I'm gonna get me a stiff bristled brush and a cake of lye soap and wash you off me."

He started up the aisle, but then stopped and turned back to her. "You are also a liar. It is your bush that you dyed to excite the customers. I smelled your hair the night you laid with your head on my chest. You ain't a redhead. I'm half in love with a real redhead and you are an insult to my thoughts of her."

She blushed and looked away from him, her fists knotted in her lap.

He found a seat as far forward as he could and sat down wearily. He stared out the window and thought, oh, Molly

182

here ain't a train can run fast enough to get me to you right now. I bad need to just sink myself down in your goodness. I am sick at heart right now and you are the only one I know that's got the honest medicine to cure me.

Then he leaned back and took a drink of whiskey. This was going to be one hell of a report to write up, and he felt sure Billy Vail would find a hundred ways to find fault with it. Then he smiled as he thought of the old curmudgeon. Hell, after what he'd been through, he'd even be glad to see that old bastard again.

After he'd stopped and seen Molly.

He took another drink and looked down at the bottle. Until then he reckoned he'd have to take what comfort was at hand.

He still didn't know if he was more angry at Janice because of the murderous trick she'd played on Carol Ann or because that flaming red bush of hers had briefly imitated Molly's. He took a drink and decided he might reduce the charges against her if she'd bleach her pubic hairs back to their normal color. She'd bleached her hair blond to surprise her customers when she undressed. He thought, Hah! Who the hell is she trying to fool. Not a deputy United States marshal who can defeat eight armed men with a little railroad flare gun.

He leaned his head back against the headrest and smiled out the window. Who the hell was he kidding? He'd got lucky as hell and he knew it. Of course that wasn't the way he was going to tell it.

Watch for

LONGARM AND THE MAN-EATERS

192nd novel in the bold LONGARM series
from Jove

Coming in December!

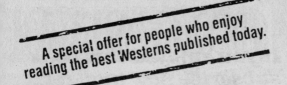